NORA ROBERTS

LESS OF A STRANGER

Harlequin Mills & Boon

First Published 1984
Second Australian Paperback Edition 2004
ISBN 0 733 55157 2

Published by
Harlequin Mills & Boon
3 Gibbes Street
CHATSWOOD NSW 2067
AUSTRALIA

Printed and bound in Australia by
McPherson's Printing Group

For my friend, Joanne

Youthful gladness, my foot! Sure, Megan Miller's family amusement park gave older folks a second youth and kids a place to play. But running Joyland was hard work, and she wasn't about to sell out to a man who was all play!

Chapter 1

He watched her coming. Though she wore jeans and a jacket, with a concealing helmet over her head, Katch recognized her femininity. She rode a small Honda motorcycle. He drew on his thin cigar and appreciated the competent way she swung into the market's parking lot.

Settling the bike, she dismounted. She was tall, Katch noted, perhaps five feet eight, and slender. He leaned back on the soda machine and continued to watch her out of idle curiosity. Then she removed the helmet. Instantly, his curiosity was intensified. She was a stunner.

Her hair was loose and straight, swinging nearly to her shoulders, with a fringe of bangs sweeping over her forehead. It was a deep, rich brunette that showed glints of red and gold from the sun. Her face was narrow, the features sharp and distinct. He'd known models who'd starved themselves to get the angles and shadows that were in this woman's face. Her mouth, however, was full and generous.

Katch recognized the subtleties of cosmetics and knew that none had been used to add interest to the woman's features. She didn't need them. Her eyes were large, and even with the distance of the parking lot between them, he caught the depth of dark brown. They reminded him of a colt's eyes—deep and wide and aware. Her movements were unaffected. They had an unrefined grace that was as coltish as her eyes. She was young, he decided, barely twenty. He drew on the cigar again. She was definitely a stunner.

"Hey, Megan!"

Megan turned at the call, brushing the

bangs from her eyes as she moved. Seeing the Bailey twins pull to the curb in their Jeep, she smiled.

"Hi." Clipping the helmet onto a strap on her bike, Megan walked to the Jeep. She was very fond of the Bailey twins.

Like herself, they were twenty-three and had golden, beach-town complexions, but they were petite, blue-eyed and pertly blonde. The long, baby-fine hair they shared had been tossed into confusion by the wind. Both pairs of blue eyes drifted past Megan to focus on the man who leaned against the soda machine. In reflex, both women straightened and tucked strands of hair behind their ears. Tacitly, they agreed their right profile was the most comely.

"We haven't seen you in a while." Teri Bailey kept one eye cocked on Katch as she spoke to Megan.

"I've been trying to get some things finished before the season starts." Megan's voice was low, with the gentle flow of coastal South Carolina. "How've you been?"

"Terrific!" Jeri answered, shifting in the driver's seat. "We've got the afternoon off.

Why don't you come shopping with us?'' She, too, kept Katch in her peripheral vision.

''I'd like to—'' Megan was already shaking her head ''—but I've got to pick up a few things here.''

''Like the guy over there with terrific gray eyes?'' Jeri demanded.

''What?'' Megan laughed.

''And shoulders,'' Teri remarked.

''He hasn't taken those eyes off her, has he, Teri?'' Jeri remarked. ''And we spent twelve-fifty for this blouse.'' She fingered the thin strap of the pink camisole top which matched her twin's.

''What,'' Megan asked, totally bewildered, ''are you talking about?''

''Behind you,'' Teri said with a faint inclination of her fair head. ''The hunk by the soda machine. Absolutely gorgeous.'' But as Megan began to turn her head, Teri continued in a desperate whisper, ''Don't turn around, for goodness sake!''

''How can I see if I don't look?'' Megan pointed out reasonably as she turned.

His hair was blond, not pale like the twins', but dusky and sun-streaked. It was thick and curled loosely and carelessly around his face. He was lean, and the jeans he wore were well faded from wear. His stance was negligent, completely relaxed as he leaned back against the machine and drank from a can. But his face wasn't lazy, Megan thought as he met her stare without a blink. It was sharply aware. He needed a shave, certainly, but his bone structure was superb. There was the faintest of clefts in his chin, and his mouth was long and thin.

Normally, Megan would have found the face fascinating—strongly sculpted, even handsome in a rough-and-ready fashion. But the eyes were insolent. They were gray, as the twins had stated, dark and smoky. And, Megan decided with a frown, rude. She'd seen his type before—drifters, loners, looking for the sun and some fleeting female companionship. Under her bangs, her eyebrows drew together. He was openly staring at her. As the can touched his lips, he sent Megan a slow wink.

Hearing one of the twins giggle, Megan whipped her head back around.

"He's adorable," Jeri decided.

"Don't be an idiot." Megan swung her

hair back with a toss of her head. ‘‘He’s typical.’’

The twins exchanged a look as Jeri started the Jeep’s engine. ‘‘Too choosy,’’ she stated. They gave Megan mirror smiles as they pulled away from the curb. ‘‘Bye!’’

Megan wrinkled her nose at them, but waved before she turned away. Purposefully ignoring the man who loitered beside the concessions, Megan walked into the market.

She acknowledged the salute from the clerk behind the counter. Megan had grown up in Myrtle Beach. She knew all the small merchants in the five-mile radius around her grandfather’s amusement park.

After choosing a basket, she began to push it down the first aisle. Just a few things, she decided, plucking a quart of milk from a shelf. She had only the saddlebags on the bike for transporting. If the truck hadn’t been acting up... She let her thoughts drift away from that particular problem. Nothing could be done about it at the moment.

Megan paused in the cookie section. She’d missed lunch and the bags and boxes looked tempting. Maybe the oatmeal...

‘‘These are better.’’

Megan started as a hand reached in front of her to choose a bag of cookies promising a double dose of chocolate chips. Twisting her head, she looked up into the insolent gray eyes.

"Want the cookies?" He grinned much as he had outside.

"No," she said, giving a meaningful glance at his hand on her basket. Shrugging, he took his hand away but, to Megan's irritation, he strolled along beside her.

"What's on the list, Meg?" he asked companionably as he tore open the bag of cookies.

"I can handle it alone, thanks." She started down the next aisle, grabbing a can of tuna. He walked, Megan noted, like a gunslinger—long, lanky strides with just a hint of swagger.

"You've got a nice bike." He bit into a cookie as he strolled along beside her. "Live around here?"

Megan chose a box of tea bags. She gave it a critical glance before tossing it into the basket. "It lives with me," she told him as she moved on.

‘‘Cute,’’ he decided and offered her a cookie. Megan ignored him and moved down the next aisle. When she reached for a loaf of bread, however, he laid a hand on top of hers. ‘‘Whole wheat’s better for you.’’ His palm was hard and firm on the back of her hand. Megan met his eyes indignantly and tried to pull away.

‘‘Listen, I have…’’

‘‘No rings,’’ he commented, lacing his fingers through hers and lifting her hand for a closer study. ‘‘No entanglements. How about dinner?’’

‘‘No way.’’ She shook her hand but found it firmly locked in his.

‘‘Don’t be unfriendly, Meg. You have fantastic eyes.’’ He smiled into them, looking at her as though they were the only two people on earth. Someone reached around her, with an annoyed mutter, to get a loaf of rye.

‘‘Will you go away?’’ she demanded in an undertone. It amazed her that his smile was having an effect on her even though she knew what was behind it. ‘‘I’ll make a scene if you don’t.’’

"That's all right," he said genially, "I don't mind scenes."

He wouldn't, she thought, eyeing him. He'd thrive on them. "Look," she began angrily, "I don't know who you are, but..."

"David Katcherton," he volunteered with another easy smile. "Katch. What time should I pick you up?"

"You're not going to pick me up," she said distinctly. "Not now, not later." Megan cast a quick look around. The market was all but empty. She couldn't cause a decent scene if she'd wanted to. "Let go of my hand," she ordered firmly.

"The Chamber of Commerce claims Myrtle Beach is a friendly town, Meg." Katch released her hand. "You're going to give them a bad name."

"And stop calling me Meg," she said furiously. "I don't know you."

She stomped off, wheeling the basket in front of her.

"You will." He made the claim quietly, but she heard him.

Their eyes met again, hers dark with temper, his assured. Turning away, she quickened her pace to the check-out counter.

* * *

"You wouldn't believe what happened at the market." Megan set the bag on the kitchen table with a thump.

Her grandfather sat at the table, on one of the four matching maple chairs, earnestly tying a fly. He grunted in acknowledgment but didn't glance up. Wires and feathers and weights were neatly piled in front of him.

"This man," she began, pulling the bread from the top bag. "This incredibly rude man tried to pick me up. Right in the cookie section." Megan frowned as she stored tea bags in a canister. "He wanted me to go to dinner with him."

"Hmm." Her grandfather meticulously attached a yellow feather to the fly. "Have a nice time."

"Pop!" Megan shook her head in frustration, but a smile tugged at her mouth.

Timothy Miller was a small, spare man in his mid-sixties. His round, lined face was tanned, surrounded by a shock of white hair and a full beard. The beard was soft as a cloud and carefully tended. His blue eyes, unfaded by the years, were settled deeply into the folds and lines of his face. They missed little. Megan could see he was focused on his lures. That he had heard her at all was a tribute to his affection for his granddaughter.

Moving over, she dropped a kiss on the crown of his head. "Going fishing tomorrow?"

"Yessiree, bright and early." Pop counted out his assortment of lures and mentally reviewed his strategy. Fishing was a serious business. "The truck should be fixed this evening. I'll be back before supper."

Megan nodded, giving him a second kiss. He needed his fishing days. The amusement parks opened for business on weekends in the spring and fall. In the three summer months they worked seven days a week. The summer kept the town alive; it drew tourists, and tourists meant business. For one-fourth of the year, the town swelled from a population of thirteen or fourteen thousand to three hundred thousand. The bulk of those three hundred thousand people had come to the small coastal town to have fun.

To provide it, and make his living, her grandfather worked hard. He always had, Megan mused. It would have been a trial if he hadn't loved the park so much. It had been part of her life for as long as she could remember.

Megan had been barely five when she had lost her parents. Over the years, Pop had been mother, father and friend to her. And Joyland was home to her as much as the beach-side cottage they lived in. Years before, they had turned to each other in grief. Now, their love was bedrock firm. With the exclusion of her grandfather, Megan was careful with her emotions, for once involved, they were intense. When she loved, she loved totally.

"Trout would be nice," she murmured, as she gave him a last, quick hug. "We'll have to settle for tuna casserole tonight."

"Thought you were going out."

"Pop!" Megan leaned back against the stove and pushed her hair from her face with both hands. "Do you think I'd spend the evening with a man who tried to pick me up with a bag of chocolate chip cookies?" With a jerk of her wrist, she flicked on the burner under the teakettle.

"Depends on the man." She saw the twinkle in his eye as he glanced up at her.

Megan knew she finally had his full attention. ''What'd he look like?''

''A beach bum,'' she retorted, although she knew the answer wasn't precisely true. ''With a bit of cowboy thrown in.'' She smiled then in response to Pop's grin. ''Actually, he had a great face. Lean and strong, very attractive in an unscrupulous sort of way. He'd do well in bronze.''

''Sounds interesting. Where'd you meet him again?''

''In the cookie section.''

''And you're going to fix tuna casserole instead of having dinner out?'' Pop gave a heavy sigh and shook his head. ''I don't know what's the matter with this girl,'' he addressed a favored lure.

''He was cocky,'' Megan claimed and folded her arms. ''And he *leered* at me. Aren't grandfathers supposed to tote shotguns around for the purpose of discouraging leerers?''

''Want to borrow one and go hunting for him?''

The shrill whistling of the kettle drowned out her response. Pop watched Megan as she rose to fix the tea.

She was a good girl, he mused. A bit too serious about things at times, but a good girl. And a beauty, too. It didn't surprise him that a stranger had tried to make a date with her. He was more surprised that it hadn't happened more often. But Megan could discourage a man without opening her mouth, he recalled. All she had to do was aim one of her "I beg your pardon" looks and most of them backed off. That seemed to be the way she wanted it.

Between the amusement park and her art, she never seemed to have time for much socializing. Or didn't make time, Pop amended thoughtfully. Still, he wasn't certain that he didn't detect more than just annoyance in her attitude toward the man in the market. Unless he missed his guess, she had been amused and perhaps a touch attracted. Because he knew his granddaughter well, he decided to let the subject ride for the time being.

"The weather's supposed to hold all weekend," he commented as he carefully placed his lures in his fishing box. "There should be a good crowd in the park. Are you going to work in the arcade?"

"Of course." Megan set two cups of tea on the table and sat again. "Have those seats been adjusted on the Ferris wheel?"

"Saw to it myself this morning." Pop blew on his tea to cool it, then sipped.

He was relaxed, Megan saw. Pop was a simple man. She'd always admired his unassuming manner, his quiet humor, his lack of pretensions. He loved to watch people enjoy. More, she added with a sigh, than he liked to charge them for doing so. Joyland never made more than a modest profit. He was, Megan concluded, a much better grandfather than businessman.

To a large extent, it was she who handled the profit-and-loss aspect of the park. Though the responsibility took time away from her art, she knew it was the park that supported them. And, more important, it was the park that Pop loved.

At the moment, the books were teetering a bit too steeply into the red for comfort. Neither of them spoke of it at any length with the other. They mentioned improvements during the busy season, talked vaguely about promoting business during the Easter break and over Memorial Day weekend.

Megan sipped at her tea and half listened to Pop's rambling about hiring summer help. She would see to it when the time came. Pop was a whiz in dealing with cranky machines and sunburned tourists, but he tended to overpay and underwork his employees. Megan was more practical. She had to be.

I'll have to work full-time myself this summer, she reflected. She thought fleetingly of the half-completed sculpture in her studio over the garage. It'll just have to wait for December, she told herself and tried not to sigh. There's no other way until things are on a more even keel again. Maybe next year…it was always next year. There were things to do, always things to do. With a small shrug, she turned back to Pop's monologue.

"So, I figure we'll get some of the usual college kids and drifters to run the rides."

"I don't imagine that'll be a problem," Megan murmured. Pop's mention of drifters had led her thoughts back to David Katcherton.

Katch, she mused, letting his face form in

her mind again. Ordinarily, she'd have cast his type as a drifter, but there had been something more than that. Megan prided herself on her observations, her characterizations of people. It annoyed her that she wasn't able to make a conclusive profile on this man. It annoyed her further that she was again thinking of a silly encounter with a rude stranger.

"Want some more tea?" Pop was already making his way to the stove when Megan shook herself back.

"Ah...yeah, sure." She scolded herself for dwelling on the insignificant when there were things to do. "I guess I'd better start dinner. You'll want an early night if you're going fishing in the morning."

"That's my girl." Pop turned the flame back on under the kettle as he glanced out the window. He cast a quick look at his unsuspecting granddaughter. "I hope you've got enough for three," he said casually. "It looks like your beach-cowboy found his way to the ranch."

"What?" Megan's brows drew together as she stood up.

"A perfect description, as usual, Megan,"

Pop complimented her as he watched the man approach, loose-limbed with a touch of a swashbuckler, a strong, good-looking face. Pop liked his looks. He turned with a grin as Megan walked to the window to stare out. Pop suppressed a chuckle at her expression.

"It *is* him," she whispered, hardly believing her eyes as she watched Katch approach her kitchen door.

"I thought it might be," Pop said mildly.

"Of all the nerve," she muttered darkly. "Of all the *incredible* nerve!"

Chapter 2

Before her grandfather could comment, Megan took the few strides necessary to bring her to the kitchen door. She swung it open just as Katch stepped up on the stoop. There was a flicker, only a flicker, of surprise in the gray eyes.

"You have a nerve," she said coolly.

"So I've been told," he agreed easily. "You're prettier than you were an hour ago." He ran a finger down her cheek. "There's a bit of rose under the honey now. Very becoming." He traced the line of her chin before dropping his hand. "Do you live here?"

"You know very well I do," she retorted. "You followed me."

Katch grinned. "Sorry to disappoint you, Meg. Finding you here's just a bonus. I'm looking for Timothy Miller. Friend of yours?"

"He's my grandfather." She moved, almost imperceptibly, positioning herself between Katch and the doorway. "What do you want with him?"

Katch recognized the protective move, but before he could comment, Pop spoke from behind her.

"Why don't you let the man in, Megan? He can tell me himself."

"I'm basically human, Meg," Katch said quietly. The tone of his voice had her looking at him more closely.

She glanced briefly over her shoulder, then turned back to Katch. The look she gave him was a warning. Don't do anything to upset him.

She noticed something in his eyes she hadn't expected—gentleness. It was more disconcerting than his earlier arrogance. Megan backed into the kitchen, holding open the door in silent invitation.

Katch smiled at her, casually brushing a strand of hair from her cheek as he walked by and into the kitchen. Megan stood for a moment, wondering why she should be so moved by a stranger's touch.

"Mr. Miller?" She heard the unaffected friendliness in Katch's voice and glanced over as he held out a hand to her grandfather. "I'm David Katcherton."

Pop nodded in approval. "You're the fellow who called me a couple of hours ago." He shot a look past Katch's shoulder to Megan. "I see you've already met my granddaughter."

His eyes smiled in response. "Yes. Charming."

Pop chuckled and moved toward the stove. "I was just about to make some more tea. How about a cup?"

Megan noticed the faint lift of his brow. Tea, she thought, was probably not his first choice.

"That'd be nice. Thanks." He walked to the table and sat, Megan decided, as if his acquaintance were long-standing and personal. Half reluctant, half defiant, she sat next to him. Her eyes asked him questions behind Pop's back.

"Did I tell you before that you have fabulous eyes?" he murmured. Without waiting for her answer, he turned his attention to Pop's tackle box. "You've got some great lures here," he observed to Pop, picking up a bone squid, then a wood plug painted to simulate a small frog. "Do you make any of your own?"

"That's half the sport," Pop stated, bringing a fresh cup to the table. "Have you done much fishing?"

"Here and there. I'd guess you'd know the best spots along the Grand Strand."

"A few of them," Pop said modestly.

Megan scowled into her tea. Once the subject of fishing had been brought up, Pop could go on for hours. And hours.

"I thought I'd do some surf casting while I'm here," Katch mentioned offhandedly. Megan was surprised to catch a shrewdly measuring expression in his eyes.

"Well now—" Pop warmed to the theme "—I might just be able to show you a spot or two. Do you have your own gear?"

"Not with me, no."

Pop brushed this off as inconsequential. "Where are you from, Mr. Katcherton?"

"Katch," he corrected, leaning back in his chair. "California originally."

That, Megan decided, explained the beachboy look. She drank her cooling tea with a casual air while studying him over the rim.

"You're a long way from home," Pop commented. He shifted comfortably, then brought out a pipe he saved for interesting conversations. "Do you plan to be in Myrtle Beach long?"

"Depends. I'd like to talk with you about your amusement park."

Pop puffed rapidly on his pipe while holding a match to the bowl. The tobacco caught, sending out cherry-scented smoke. "So you said on the phone. Funny, Megan and I were just talking about hiring on help for the summer. Only about six weeks before the season starts." He puffed and let the smoke waft lazily. "Less than three until Easter. Ever worked rides or a booth?"

"No." Katch sampled his tea.

"Well..." Pop shrugged his inexperience

away. ‘‘It’s simple enough to learn. You look smart.’’ Again, Megan caught the flash of Katch’s grin. She set down her cup.

‘‘We can’t pay more than minimum to a novice,’’ she said dampeningly.

He made her nervous, she was forced to admit. With any luck, she could discourage him from Joyland so that he’d try his luck elsewhere. But something nagged at her. He didn’t look the type to take a job running a roller coaster or hawking a pitch-and-toss for a summer. There were hints of authority in his face, touches of casual power in his stance. Yet there was something not altogether respectable in his raffish charm.

He met her stare with a complete lack of self-consciousness. ‘‘That seems reasonable. Do you work in the park, Meg?’’

She bit back a retort to his familiarity. ‘‘Often,’’ she said succinctly.

‘‘Megan’s got a good business head,’’ Pop interjected. ‘‘She keeps me straight.’’

‘‘Funny,’’ Katch said speculatively. ‘‘Somehow I thought you might be a model. You’ve the face for it.’’ There was no flirtatiousness in his tone.

"Megan's an artist," Pop said, puffing contentedly at his pipe.

"Oh?"

She watched Katch's eyes narrow and focus on her. Uncomfortable, she shifted in her chair. "We seem to be drifting away from the subject," she said crisply. "If you've come about a job—"

"No."

"But...didn't you say—"

"I don't think so," he cut her off again and added a smile. He turned to Pop now, and Megan recognized a subtle change in his manner. "I don't want a job in your park, Mr. Miller. I want to buy it."

Both men were intent on each other. Pop was surprised, unmistakably so, but there was also a look of consideration in his eyes. Neither of them noticed Megan. She stared at Katch, her face open and young, and just a little frightened. She wanted to laugh and say he was making a foolish joke, but she knew better. Katch said exactly what he meant.

She'd recognized the understated authority and power beneath the glib exterior. This was business, pure and simple. She could see it on his face. There was a flutter of panic in her stomach as she looked at her grandfather.

"Pop?" Her voice was very small, and he made no sign that he heard her.

"You're a surprise," the old man said eventually. Then he began to puff on his pipe again. "Why my park?"

"I've done some research on the amusements here." Katch shrugged off the details. "I like yours."

Pop sighed and blew smoke at the ceiling. "I can't say I'm interested in selling out, son. A man gets used to a certain way of life."

"With the offer I'm prepared to make, you might find it easy to get used to another."

Pop gave a quiet laugh. "How old are you, Katch?"

"Thirty-one."

"That's just about how long I've been in this business. How much do you know about running a park?"

"Not as much as you do." Katch grinned and leaned back again. "But I could learn fast with the right teacher."

Megan saw that her grandfather was studying Katch carefully. She felt excluded from the conversation and resented it. Her grandfather was capable of doing this very subtly. She recognized that David Katcherton had the same talent. Megan sat silently; natural courtesy forbade her interrupting private conversation.

"Why do you want to own an amusement park?" Pop asked suddenly. Megan could tell he was interested in David Katcherton. A warning bell began to ring in her head. The last thing she wanted was for her grandfather to become too involved with Katch. He was trouble, Megan was sure of it.

"It's good business," Katch answered Pop's question after a moment. "And fun." He smiled. "I like things that put fun into life."

He knows how to say the right thing, Megan acknowledged grudgingly, noting Pop's expression.

"I'd appreciate it if you'd think about it, Mr. Miller," Katch continued. "We could talk about it again in a few days."

And how to advance and retreat, she thought.

"I can't refuse to think about it," Pop agreed, but shook his head. "Still, you might take another look around. Megan and I've run Joyland for a good many years. It's home to us." He looked to his granddaughter teasingly. "Weren't you two going out to dinner?"

"No!" She flashed him a scowl.

"Exactly what I had in mind," Katch said smoothly. "Come on, Meg, I'll buy you a hamburger." As he rose, he took her hand, pulling her to her feet. Feeling her temper rise with her, Megan attempted to control it.

"I can't tell you how I hate to refuse such a charming invitation," she began.

"Then don't," Katch cut her off before turning to Pop. "Would you like to join us?"

Pop chuckled and motioned them away with the back of his hand. "Go on. I've got to get my gear together for the morning."

"Want company?"

Pop studied Katch over the bowl of his pipe. "I'm leaving at five-thirty," he said after a moment. "I have extra gear."

"I'll be here."

Megan was so astonished that she allowed

Katch to lead her outside without making another protest. Pop never invited anyone along on his fishing mornings. They were his relaxation, and he enjoyed his solitude too much to share it.

"He never takes anyone with him," she murmured, thinking aloud.

"Then I'm flattered."

Megan noticed that Katch still had her hand, his fingers comfortably laced with hers.

"I'm not going out with you," she said positively and stopped walking. "You might be able to charm Pop into taking you fishing, but—"

"So you think I'm charming?" His smile was audacious as he took her other hand.

"Not in the least," she said firmly, repressing an answering smile.

"Why won't you have dinner with me?"

"Because," she said, meeting his eyes directly, "I don't like you."

His smile broadened. "I'd like the chance to change your mind."

"You couldn't." Megan started to draw her hands away, but he tightened his fingers.

"Wanna bet?" Again, she squashed the

desire to smile. ''If I change your mind, you'll go to the park with me Friday night.''

''And if I don't change my mind?'' she asked. ''What then?''

''I won't bother you anymore.'' He grinned, as persuasive, she noted, as he was confident.

Her brow lifted in speculation. It might, she reflected, it just might be worth it.

''All you have to do is have dinner with me tonight,'' Katch continued, watching Megan's face. ''Just a couple of hours.''

''All right,'' she agreed impulsively. ''It's a deal.'' She wriggled her fingers, but he didn't release them. ''We could shake on it,'' she said, ''but you still have my hands.''

''So I do,'' he agreed. ''We'll seal it my way then.''

With a quick tug, he had her colliding against his chest. She felt a strength there which wasn't apparent in the lean, somewhat lanky frame. Before she could express annoyance, his mouth had taken hers.

He was skillful and thorough. She never knew whether she had parted her lips instinctively or if he had urged her to do so with the gently probing tip of his tongue.

From the instant of contact, Megan's mind had emptied, to be filled only with thoughts she couldn't center on. Her body dominated, taking command in simple surrender. She was melted against him, aware of his chest hard against her breasts…aware of his mouth quietly savaging hers. There was nothing else. She found there was nothing to hold on to. No anchor to keep her from veering off into wild water. Megan gave a small, protesting moan and drew away.

His eyes were darker than she'd thought, and too smoky to read clearly. Why had she thought them so decipherable? Why had she thought him so manageable? Nothing was as she had thought it had been minutes before. Her breath trembled as she fought to collect herself.

"You're very warm," Katch said softly. "It's a pity you struggle so hard to be remote."

"I'm not. I don't…" Megan shook her head, wishing desperately for her heartbeat to slow.

"You are," he corrected, "and you do." Katch gave her hands a companionable squeeze before releasing one of them. The other he kept snugly in his as he turned toward his car.

Panic was welling up inside Megan, and she tried to suppress it. *You've been kissed before,* she reminded herself. This was just unexpected. It just caught you off guard. Even as the excuse ran through her mind, she knew it for a lie. She'd never been kissed like that before. And the situation was no longer under her control.

"I don't think I'll go after all," she told him in calmer tones.

Katch turned, smiling at her as he opened the car door. "A bet's a bet, Meg."

Chapter 3

Katch drove a black Porsche. Megan wasn't surprised. She wouldn't have expected him to drive anything ordinary. It wasn't difficult to deduce that David Katcherton could afford the best of everything.

He'd probably inherited his money, she decided as she settled back against the silver gray seat cushion. He'd probably never worked a day in his life. She remembered the hard, unpampered feel of his palm. Probably a whiz at sports, she thought. Plays tennis, squash, sails his own yacht. Never does anything worthwhile. Only looks for pleasure. *And finds it,* she thought.

Megan turned to him, pushing her swinging hair back behind her shoulders. His profile was sharply attractive, with the dusky blond hair curling negligently over his ear.

"See something you like?"

Megan flushed in annoyance, aware that she'd been caught staring.

"You need a shave," she said primly.

Katch turned the rearview mirror toward him as if to check her analysis. "Guess I do." He smiled as they merged into the traffic. "On our next date I'll be sure to remember. Don't say anything," he added, feeling her stiffen at his side. "Didn't your mother ever tell you not to say anything if you couldn't say something pleasant?"

Megan stifled a retort.

Katch smiled as he merged into traffic. "How long have you lived here?"

"Always." With the windows down, Megan could hear the outdoor noises. The music from a variety of car radios competed against each other and merged into a strange sort of harmony. Megan liked the cluttered, indefinable sound. She felt herself relaxing and straightened her shoulders and faced Katch again.

"And what do you do?"

He caught the thread of disdain in the question, but merely lifted a brow. "I own things."

"Really? What sort of things?"

Katch stopped at a red light, then turned, giving her a long, direct look. "Anything I want." The light changed and he deftly slid the car into the parking lot.

"We can't go in there," Megan told him with a glance at the exclusive restaurant.

"Why not?" Katch switched off the ignition. "The food's good here."

"I know, but we're not dressed properly, and—"

"Do you like doing things properly all the time, Meg?"

The question stopped her. She searched his face carefully, wondering if he was laughing at her, and unsure of the answer.

"Tell you what." He eased himself out of the car, then leaned back in the window. "Think about it for a few minutes. I'll be back."

Megan watched him slide through the elegant doors of the restaurant and shook her head. They'll boot him out, she thought. Still, she couldn't help admiring his confidence. There was something rather elusive about it. She crossed her arms over. "Still, I don't really *like* him," she muttered.

Fifteen minutes later, she decided she liked him even less. How impossibly rude! she fumed as she slammed out of his car. Keeping me waiting out here all this time!

She decided to find the nearest phone booth and call her grandfather to ask him to come pick her up. She searched the pockets in her jeans and her jacket. Not a dime, she thought furiously. Not one thin dime to my name. Taking a deep breath, she stared at the doors of the restaurant. She'd have to borrow change, or beg their permission to use the house phone. Anything was better than waiting in the car. Just as she pulled open the door of the restaurant, Katch strolled out.

"Thanks," he said casually and moved past her.

Megan stared after him. He was carrying the biggest picnic basket she'd ever seen.

After he'd opened the trunk and settled it inside, he glanced back up at her.

"Well come on." He slammed the lid. "I'm starving."

"What's in there?" she asked suspiciously.

"Dinner." He motioned for her to get in the car. Megan stood beside the closed door on the passenger side.

"How did you get them to do that?"

"I asked. Are you hungry?"

"Well, yes... But how—"

"Then let's go." Katch dropped into the driver's seat and started the engine. The moment she sat beside him, he swung out of the parking lot. "Where's your favorite place?" he demanded.

"My favorite place?" she repeated dumbly.

"You can't tell me you've lived here all your life and don't have a favorite place." Katch turned the car toward the ocean. "Where is it?"

"Toward the north end of the beach," she said. "Not many people go there, except at the height of the season."

"Good. I want to be alone with you."

The simple directness had butterflies dancing in her stomach. Slowly, she turned to look at him again.

"Anything wrong with that?" The smile was back, irreverent and engaging. Megan sighed, feeling like she was just climbing the first hill of a roller coaster.

"Probably," she murmured.

The beach was deserted but for the crying gulls. She stood for a moment facing west, enjoying the rich glow of the dying sun.

"I love this time of day," she said softly. "Everything seems so still. As if the day's holding its breath." She jumped when Katch's hands came to her shoulders.

"Easy," he murmured, kneading the suddenly tense muscles as he stood behind her. He looked over her head to the sunset. "I like it just before dawn, when the birds first start to sing and the light's still soft.

"You should relax more often," he told her. He slid his fingers lazily up her neck and down again. The pleasure became less quiet and more demanding. When she would have slipped away, Katch turned her to face him.

"No," she said immediately, "don't." Megan placed both her hands on his chest. "Don't."

"All right." He relaxed his hold, but didn't release her for a moment. Then he stooped for the picnic basket and pulled out a white tablecloth saying briskly, "Besides, it's time to eat." Megan took it from him, marveling that the restaurant had given him their best linen.

"Here you go." With his head still bent over the basket, he handed her the glasses.

And their crystal, she thought, dazed as she accepted the elegant wineglasses. There was china next, then silver.

"Why did they give you all this?"

"They were low on paper plates."

"Champagne?" She glanced at the label as he poured. "You must be crazy!"

"What's the matter?" he returned mildly. "Don't you like champagne?"

"Actually I do, though I've only had American."

"Here's to the French." Katch held out a glass to her.

Megan sipped. "It's wonderful," she said before experimenting with another sip. "But you didn't have to..." she gestured expansively.

"I decided I wasn't in the mood for a hamburger." Katch screwed the bottle down into the sand. He placed a small container on the cloth, then dived back into the basket.

"What's this?" Megan demanded as she opened it. She frowned at the shiny black mass inside. He placed toast points on a plate. "Is it..." She paused in disbelief and glanced at him. "Is this caviar?"

"Yeah. Let me have some, will you? I'm starving." Katch took it from her and spread a generous amount on a piece of toast. "Don't you want any?" he asked her as he took a bite.

"I don't know." Megan examined it critically. "I've never tasted it before."

"No?" He offered her his piece. "Taste it." When she hesitated, Katch grinned and held it closer to her mouth. "Go on, Meg, have a bite."

"It's salty," she said with surprise. She plucked the toast from his hand and took another bite. "And it's good," she decided, swallowing.

"You might've left me some," he complained when Megan finished off the toast. She laughed and, heaping caviar onto another piece, handed it to him. "I wondered how it would sound." Katch took the offering, but his attention was on Megan.

"What?" Still smiling, she licked a bit of caviar from her thumb.

"Your laugh. I wondered if it would be as appealing as your face." He took a bite now, still watching her. "It is."

Megan tried to calm her fluttering pulse. "You didn't have to feed me caviar and champagne to hear me laugh." With a casual shrug, she moved out of his reach. "I laugh quite a bit."

"Not often enough."

She looked back at him in surprise. "Why do you say that?"

"Your eyes are so serious. So's your mouth." His glance swept over her face. "Perhaps that's why I feel compelled to make you smile."

"How extraordinary." Megan sat back on her heels and stared at him. "You barely know me."

"Does it matter?"

"I always thought it should," she murmured as he reached into the hamper again. Megan watched, no longer surprised as he drew out lobster tails and fresh strawberries. She laughed again and, pushing back her hair, moved closer to him.

"Here," she said. "Let me help."

The sun sank as they ate. The moon rose. It shot a shimmering white line across the sea. Megan thought it was like a dream—the china and silver gleaming in the moonlight, the exotic tastes on her tongue, the familiar sound of surf and the stranger beside her, who was becoming less of a stranger every minute.

Already Megan knew the exact movement of his face when he smiled, the precise tonal quality of his voice. She knew the exact pattern of the curls over his ear. More than once, bewitched by moonlight and champagne, she had to restrain her fingers from reaching for them, experimenting with them.

"Aren't you going to eat any cheesecake?" Katch gestured with a forkful, then slid it into his mouth.

"I can't." Megan brought her knees up to her chest and rested her chin on them. She watched his obvious enjoyment with dessert. "How do you do it?"

"Dedication." Katch took the last bite. "I try to see every project through to the finish."

"I've never had a picnic like this," she told him with a contented sigh. Leaning back on her elbows, she stretched out her legs and looked up at the stars. "I've never tasted anything so wonderful."

"I'll give Ricardo your compliments." Katch moved to sit beside her. His eyes moved from the crown of her head down the slender arch of her neck. Her face was thrown up to the stars.

"Who's Ricardo?" she asked absently. There was no thought of objection when Katch tucked her hair behind her ear with his fingertip.

"The chef. He loves compliments."

Megan smiled, liking the way the sound of his voice mixed with the sound of the sea. "How do you know?"

"That's how I lured him away from Chicago."

"Lured him away? What do you mean?"

It took only an instant for the answer to come to her. "You own that restaurant?"

"Yes." He smiled at the incredulity in her face. "I bought it a couple of years ago."

Megan glanced at the white linen cloth scattered with fine china and heavy silver. She recalled that a little more than two years before, the restaurant had been ready to go under. The food had been overpriced and the service slack. Then it had received a face-lift. The interior had been redesigned, boasting, she was told, a mirrored ceiling. Since its reopening, it had maintained the highest of reputations in a town which prided itself on its quality and variety of restaurants.

She shifted her attention back to him. "*You* bought it?"

"That's right." Katch smiled at her. He sat Indian-style, facing her as she leaned back on her elbows. "Does that surprise you?"

Megan looked at him carefully: the careless toss of curls, the white knees of his jeans, the frayed sneakers. He was not her conception of a successful businessman. Where was the three-piece suit, the careful hairstyling? And yet…she had to admit there was something in his face.

"No," she said at length. "No, I suppose it doesn't." Megan frowned as he shifted his position. In a moment he was close, facing the sea as she did. "You bought it the same way you want to buy Joyland."

"I told you, that's what I do."

"But it's more than owning things, isn't it?" she insisted, not satisfied with his offhand answers. "It's making a success of them."

"That's the idea," he agreed. "There's a certain satisfaction in succeeding, don't you think?"

Megan sat up and turned to him. "But you can't have Joyland, it's Pop's whole life. You don't understand…"

"Maybe not," he said easily. "You can explain it to me later. Not tonight." He covered her hand with his. "This isn't a night for business."

"Katch, you have to—"

"Look at the stars, Meg," he suggested as he did so himself. "Have you ever tried to count them?"

Her eyes were irresistibly drawn upward. "When I was little. But—"

"Star counting isn't just for kids," he instructed in a voice warm and laced with humor. "Do you come here at night?"

The stars were brilliant and low over the sea. "Sometimes," she murmured. "When a project isn't going well and I need to clear my head, or just be alone."

"What sort of artist are you?" His fingers trailed over her knuckles. "Do you paint seascapes? Portraits?"

She smiled and shook her head. "No, I sculpt."

"Ah." He lifted her hand, then examined it—one side, then the other—while she watched him. "Yes, I can see that. Your hands are strong and capable." When he pressed his lips to the center of her palm, she felt the jolt shoot through her entire body.

Carefully, Megan drew her hand away; then, bringing her knees up to her chest, wrapped her arms around them. She could feel Katch smile without seeing it.

"What do you work in? Clay, wood, stone?"

"All three." Turning her head, she smiled again.

"Where did you study?"

"I took courses in college." With a shrug, she passed this off. "There hasn't been much time for it." She looked up at the sky again. "The moon's so white tonight. I like to come here when it's full like this, so that the light's silvery."

When his lips brushed her ear, she would have jerked away, but he slipped an arm around her shoulders. "Relax, Meg." His voice was a whisper at her cheek. "There's a moon and the ocean. That's all there is besides us."

With his lips tingling on her skin, she could almost believe him. Her limbs were heavy, drugged with wine and the magic of his touch. Katch trailed his mouth down to her throat so that she moaned with the leap of her pulse.

"Katch, I'd better go." He was tracing her jaw with light kisses. "Please," she said weakly.

"Later," he murmured, going back to nuzzle her ear. "Much, much later."

"No, I..." Megan turned her head, and the words died.

Her lips were no more than a breath from his. She stared at him, eyes wide and aware as he bent closer. Still his mouth didn't touch hers. It hovered, offering, promising. She moaned again, lids lowering as he teased the corners of her lips. His hands never touched her. He had moved his arm so that their only contact was his mouth and tongue on her skin and the mingling of their breath.

Megan felt her resistance peel away, layer by layer until there was only need. She forgot to question the dangers, the consequences. She could only feel. Her mouth sought his. There was no hesitation or shyness now but demand, impatient demand, as she hungered to feel what she had felt before—the delicious confusion, the dark awareness.

When he still didn't touch her, Megan slipped her arms around him. She pulled him close, enjoying his soft sound of pleasure as the kiss deepened. Still, he let her lead, touching her now, but lightly, his fingers in her hair. She could barely hear the hissing of the surf over the pounding of her heart. Finally, she drew away, pulling in a deep breath as their lips separated.

But he wouldn't let her go. "Again?" The question was quiet and seemed to shout through the still night.

Refusal trembled on Megan's tongue. She knew the ground beneath her was far from solid. His hand on the back of her neck brought her a whisper closer.

"Yes," she said, and went into his arms.

This time he was less passive. He showed her there were many ways to kiss. Short and light, long and deep. Tongue and teeth and lips could all bring pleasure. Together, they lowered themselves to the sand.

It was a rough blanket, but she felt only the excitement of his lips on her skin as they wandered to her throat. She ran her fingers through his hair. His mouth returned to hers, harder now, more insistent. She was ready for it, answering it. Craving it.

When his hand took the naked skin of her breast, she murmured in resistance. She hadn't felt him release the zipper of her jacket or the buttons of her shirt. But his hand was gentle, persuasive. He let his fingers trail over her, a whispering touch. Resistance melted into surrender, then heated into passion. It was smoldering just under her skin, threatening to explode into something out of her control. She moved under him and his hands became less gentle.

There was a hunger in the kiss now. She could taste it, a flavor sharper than any she'd known. It was more seductive than soft words or champagne, and more frightening.

"I want you." Katch spoke against her mouth, but the words were not in his easygoing tone. "I want to make love with you."

Megan felt control slipping from her grasp. Her need for him was overpowering, her appetite ravenous. She struggled to climb back to reality, to remember who they were. Names, places, responsibilities. There was more than the moon and the sea. And he was a stranger, a man she barely knew.

"No." Megan managed to free her mouth from his. She struggled to her feet. "No." The repetition was shaky. Quickly, she began to fumble with the buttons of her shirt.

Katch stood and gathered the shirttail in his hands. Surprised, Megan looked up at him. His eyes were no longer calm, but his voice was deadly so. ''Why not?''

Megan swallowed. There wasn't lazy arrogance here, but a hint of ruthlessness. She had sensed it, but seeing it was much more potent. ''I don't want to.''

''Liar,'' he said simply.

''All right.'' She nodded, conceding his point. ''I don't know you.''

Katch inclined his head in agreement but tugged on the tails of her shirt to bring her closer. ''You will,'' he assured her. He kissed her then, searingly. ''But we'll wait until you do.''

She fought to steady her breathing and stabilize her pulse. ''Do you think you should always get what you want?'' she demanded. The defiance was back, calming her.

''Yes,'' he said and grinned. ''Of course.''

''You're going to be disappointed.'' She smacked his hands from her shirt and began doing the buttons. Her fingers were unfaltering. ''You can't have Joyland and you can't have me. Neither of us is for sale.''

The roughness with which he took her

arm had her eyes flying back to his face. "I don't buy women." He was angry, his eyes dark with it. The appealing voice had hardened like flint. The artist in her was fascinated by the planes of his face, the woman was uneasy with his harsh tone. "I don't have to. We're both aware that with a bit more persuasion I'd have had you tonight."

Megan pulled out of his hold. "What happened tonight doesn't mean I find you irresistible, you know." She zipped up her jacket with one quick jerk. "I can only repeat, you can't have Joyland and you can't have me."

Katch watched her a moment as she stood in the moonlight, her back to the sea. The smile came again, slowly, arrogantly. "I'll have you both, Meg," he promised quietly. "Before the season begins."

Chapter 4

The afternoon sun poured into Megan's studio. She was oblivious to it, and to the birdsong outside the windows. Her mind was focused on the clay her hands worked with, or, more precisely, on what she saw in the partially formed mound.

She had put her current project aside, something she rarely did, to begin a new one. The new subject had haunted her throughout the night. She would exorcise David Katcherton by doing a bust of him.

Megan could see it clearly, knew precisely what she wanted to capture: strength and determination behind a surface affability.

Though she had yet to admit it, Katch had frightened her the night before. Not physically—he was too intelligent to use brute force, she acknowledged—but by the force of his personality. Angrily, she stabbed at the clay. Obviously, this was a man who got what he wanted. But she was determined that this time he would not have his way. He would soon find out that she couldn't be pushed around any more than Pop could. Slowly and meticulously, her fingers worked to mold the planes of his face. It gave her a certain satisfaction to have control over him—if only vicariously with the clay.

Almost without thinking, she shaped a careless curl over the high brow. She stepped back to survey it. Somehow, she had caught a facet of his nature. He was a rogue, she decided. The old-fashioned word suited him. She could picture him with boots and six-guns, dealing cards for stud poker in a Tucson saloon; with a saber, captaining a ship into the Barbary Coast. Her fingers absently caressed the clay curls. He would laugh in the face of the wind, take treasure and women where he found them. *Women.* Megan's thoughts zeroed in on the night before.... On the feel of his lips on hers, the touch of his hand on her skin. She could remember the texture of the sand as they had lain together, the scent and sounds of the sea. And she remembered how the moonlight had fallen on his hair, how her hands had sought it while his lips had wandered over her. How thick and soft it had felt. How...

Megan stopped, appalled. She glanced down to see her fingers in the clay replica of Katch's hair. She swore, and nearly, very nearly, reduced the clay to a formless mass. Controlling herself, she rose, backing away from the forming bust. I should never allow myself to be distracted from my work by petty annoyances, she thought. Her evening with Katch belonged in that category. Just a petty annoyance. Not important.

But it was difficult for Megan to convince herself this was true. Both her intuition and her emotions told her that Katch was important, far more important than a stranger should be to a sensible woman.

And I *am* sensible, she reminded herself.

Taking a long breath, she moved to the basin to rinse the clay from her hands. She had to be sensible. Pop needed someone around to remind him that bills had to be paid. A smile crept across her mouth as she dried her hands. Megan thought, as she did from time to time, that she had been almost as much of a savior to her grandfather as he had been to her.

In the beginning, she'd been so young, so dependent upon him. And he hadn't let her down. Then, as she had grown older, Megan had helped by assuming the duties her grandfather had found tiresome: accounts and bank reconciliations. Often, Megan suppressed her own desires in order to fulfill what she thought of as her duty. She dealt with figures, the unromantic process of adding and subtracting. But she also dealt with the illusionary world of art. There were times, when she was deep in her work, that she forgot the rules she had set up for day-to-day living. Often she felt pulled in two directions. She had enough to think about without David Katcherton.

Why a man virtually unknown to her should so successfully upset the delicate balance of her world, she didn't know. She shook her head. Instead of dwelling on it, she decided, she would work out her frustration by finishing the bust. When it was done, perhaps she would be able to see more clearly exactly how she perceived him. She returned to her work.

The next hour passed quickly. She forgot her irritation with Katch for going fishing with her grandfather. How annoying to have seen him so eager and well rested when she had peeked through her bedroom curtain at five-thirty that morning! She'd fallen back into her rumpled bed to spend another hour staring, heavy-eyed, at the ceiling. She refused to remember how appealing his laugh had sounded in the hush of dawn.

The planes of his face were just taking shape under her hands when she heard a car drive up. Katch's laugh was followed by the more gravelly tones of her grandfather's.

Because her studio was above the garage, Megan had a bird's-eye view of the house and drive. She watched as Katch lifted their fishing cooler from the back of the pickup. A grin was on his face, but whatever he said was too low for Megan to hear. Pop threw back his head, his dramatic mane of white flying back as he roared his appreciation. He gave Katch a companionable slap on the back. Unaccountably, Megan was miffed. They seemed to be getting along entirely too well.

She continued to watch the man as they unloaded tackle boxes and gear. Katch was dressed much as he had been the day before. The pale blue T-shirt had lettering across the chest, but the words were faded and the distance was too great for Megan to read them. He wore Pop's fishing cap, another source of annoyance for Megan. She was forced to admit the two of them looked good together. There was the contrast between their ages and their builds, but both seemed to her to be extraordinarily masculine men. Their looks were neither smooth nor pampered. She became engrossed with the similarities and differences between them. When Katch looked up, spotting her at the window, Megan continued to stare down, oblivious, absorbed with what she saw in them.

Katch grinned, pushing the fishing cap back so that he had a clearer view. The window was long, the sill coming low at her knees. It had the effect of making Megan seem to be standing in a full-size picture frame. As was her habit when working, she had pulled her hair back in a ribbon. Her face seemed younger and more vulnerable, her eyes wider. The ancient shirt of Pop's she used as a smock dwarfed her.

Her eyes locked on Katch's, and for a moment she thought she saw something flash in them—something she'd seen briefly the night before in the moonlight. A response trembled along her skin. Then his grin was arrogant again, his eyes amused.

"Come on down, Meg." He gestured before he bent to lift the cooler again. "We brought you a present." He turned to carry the cooler around the side of the house.

"I'd rather have emeralds," she called back.

"Next time," Katch promised carelessly, before turning to carry the cooler around the side of the house.

She found Katch alone, setting up for the cleaning of the catch. He smiled when he saw her and set down the knife he held, then pulled her into his arms and kissed her thoroughly, to her utter astonishment. It was a kiss of casual ownership rather than passion, but it elicited a response that surprised her with its force. More than a little shaken, Megan pushed away.

"You can't just..."

"I already did," he pointed out. "You've been working," Katch stated as if the searing kiss had never taken place. "I'd like to see your studio."

It was better, Megan decided, to follow his lead and keep the conversation light. "Where's my grandfather?" she asked as she moved to the cooler and prepared to lift the lid.

"Pop's inside stowing the gear."

Though it was the habit of everyone who knew him to refer to Timothy Miller as Pop, Megan frowned at Katch.

"You work fast, don't you?"

"Yes, I do. I like your grandfather, Meg. You of all people should understand how easy that is to do."

Megan regarded him steadily. She took a step closer, as if testing the air between them. "I don't know if I should trust you."

"You shouldn't." Katch grinned again

and ran a finger down the bridge of her nose. "Not for a second." He tossed open the lid of the cooler, then gestured to the fish inside. "Hungry?"

Megan smiled, letting herself be charmed despite the warnings of her sensible self. "I wasn't. But I could be. Especially if I don't have to clean them."

"Pop told me you were squeamish."

"Oh, he *did,* did he?" Megan cast a long, baleful look over her shoulder toward the house. "What else did he tell you?"

"That you like daffodils and used to have a stuffed elephant named Henry."

Megan's mouth dropped open. "He told you that?"

"And that you watch horror movies, then sleep with the blankets over your head."

Megan narrowed her eyes as Katch's grin widened. "Excuse me," she said crossly, pushing Katch aside before racing through the kitchen door. She could hear Katch's laughter behind her.

"Pop!" She found him in the narrow room off the kitchen where he stored his fishing paraphernalia. He gave her an affectionate smile as she stood, hands on hips, in the doorway.

"Hi, Megan. Let me tell you, that boy knows how to fish. Yessiree, he knows how to fish."

His obvious delight with Katch caused Megan to clench her teeth. "That's the best news I've had all day," she said, stepping into the room. "But exactly why did you feel it necessary to tell *that boy* that I had a stuffed elephant and slept with the covers over my head?"

Pop lifted a hand, ostensibly to scratch his head. It wasn't in time, however, to conceal the grin. Megan's brows drew together.

"Pop, really," she said in exasperation. "Must you babble about me as if I were a little girl?"

"You'll always be my little girl," he said maddeningly, and kissed her cheek. "Did you see those trout? We'll have a heck of a fish fry tonight."

"I suppose," Megan began and folded her arms, "*he's* going to eat with us."

"Well, of course." Pop blinked his eyes. "After all, Meg, he caught half the fish."

"That's just peachy."

"We thought you might whip up some of your special blueberry tarts." He smiled ingenuously.

Megan sighed, recognizing defeat.

Within minutes, Pop heard the thumping and banging of pans. He grinned, then slipped out of the room, moving noiselessly through the house and out the front door.

"Whip up some tarts," Megan muttered later as she cut shortening into the flour. "*Men.*"

She was bending over to slip the pastry shells into the oven when the screen door slammed shut behind her. Turning, she brushed at the seat of her pants and met the predictable grin.

"I've heard about your tarts," Katch commented, setting the cleaned, filleted fish on the counter. "Pop said he had a few things to see to in the garage and to call him when dinner's ready."

Megan glared through the screen door at the adjoining building. "Oh, he did, did he?" She turned back to Katch. "Well, if you think you can just sit back and be waited on, then you're in for a disappointment."

"You didn't think I'd allow you to cook my fish, did you?" he interrupted.

She stared at his unperturbed face.

"I always cook my own fish. Where's the frying pan?"

Silently, still eyeing him, Megan pointed out the cabinet. She watched as he squatted down to rummage for it.

"It's not that I don't think you're a good cook," he went on as he stood again with the cast-iron skillet in his hand. "It's that I know I am."

"Are you implying I couldn't cook those pathetic little sardines properly?"

"Let's just say I just don't like to take chances with my dinner." He began poking into cupboards. "Why don't you make a salad," he suggested mildly, "and leave the fish to me?" There was a grunt of approval as he located the cracker meal.

Megan watched him casually going through her kitchen cupboards. "Why don't you," she began, "take your trout and..."

Her suggestion was interrupted by the rude buzz of the oven timer.

"Your tarts." Katch walked to the refrigerator for eggs and milk.

With supreme effort, Megan controlled herself enough to deal with the pastry shells. Setting them on the rack to cool, she decided to create the salad of the decade. It would put his pan-fried trout to shame.

For a time there were no words. The hot oil hissed as Katch added his coated trout. Megan tore the lettuce. She sliced raw vegetables. The scent from the pan was enticing. Megan peeled a carrot and sighed. Hearing her, Katch raised a questioning eyebrow.

"You had to be good at it, didn't you?" Megan's smile was reluctant. "You had to do it right."

He shrugged, then snatched the peeled carrot from her hand. "You'd like it better if I didn't?" Katch took a bite of the carrot before Megan could retrieve it. Shaking her head, she selected another.

"It would have been more gratifying if you'd fumbled around and made a mess of things."

Katch tilted his head as he poked at the sizzling fish with a spatula. "Is that a compliment?"

Megan diced the carrot, frowning at it thoughtfully. "I don't know. It might be easier to deal with you if you didn't seem so capable."

He caught her off guard by taking her shoulders and turning her around to face him. "Is that what you want to do?" His fingers gently massaged her flesh. "Deal with me?" When she felt herself being drawn closer, she placed her hands on his chest. "Do I make you nervous?"

"No." Megan shook her head with the denial. "No, of course not." Katch only lifted a brow and drew her closer. "Yes," she admitted in a rush, and pulled away. "Yes, blast it, you do." Stalking to the refrigerator, she yanked out the blueberry filling she had prepared. "You needn't look so pleased about it," she told him, wishing she could work up the annoyance she thought she should feel.

"Several things make me nervous." Megan moved to the pastry shells and began to spoon in the filling. "Snakes, tooth decay, large unfriendly dogs." When she heard him chuckle, Megan turned her head and found herself grinning at him. "It's difficult to actively dislike you when you make me laugh."

“Do you have to actively dislike me?” Katch flipped the fish expertly and sent oil sizzling.

“That was my plan,” Megan admitted. “It seemed like a good idea.”

“Why don’t we work on a different plan?” Katch suggested, searching through a cupboard again for a platter. “What do you like? Besides daffodils?”

“Soft ice cream,” Megan responded spontaneously. “Oscar Wilde, walking barefoot.”

“How about baseball?” Katch demanded.

Megan paused in the act of filling the shells. “What about it?”

“Do you like it?”

“Yes,” she considered, smiling. “As a matter of fact, I do.”

“I knew we had something in common.” Katch grinned. He turned the flame off under the pan. “Why don’t you call Pop? The fish is done.”

There was something altogether too cozy about the three of them sitting around the kitchen table eating a meal each of them had a part in providing, Megan thought. She could sense the growing affection between the two men and it worried her. She was sure that Katch was still as determined as ever to buy Joyland. Yet Pop was so obviously happy in his company. Megan decided that, while she couldn't trust Katch unreservedly, neither could she maintain her original plan. She couldn't dislike him or keep him from touching their lives. She thought it best not to dwell on precisely how he was touching hers.

"Tell you what." Pop sighed over his empty plate and leaned back in his chair. "Since the pair of you cooked dinner, I'll do the dishes." His eyes passed over Megan to Katch. "Why don't you two go for a walk? Megan likes to walk on the beach."

"Pop!"

"I know you young people like to be alone," he continued shamelessly.

Megan opened her mouth to protest, but Katch spoke first. "I'm always willing to take a walk with a beautiful woman, especially if it means getting out of KP," he said.

"You have such a gracious way of putting things," Megan began.

"Actually, I'd really like to see your studio."

"Take Katch up, Megan," Pop insisted. "I've been bragging about your pieces all day. Let him see for himself."

After a moment's hesitation, Megan decided it was simpler to agree. Certainly she didn't mind showing Katch her work. And, there was little doubt that it was safer to let him putter around her studio than to walk with him on the beach.

"All right." She rose. "I'll take you up."

As they passed through the screen door, Katch slipped his arm over her shoulders. "This is a nice place," he commented. He looked around the small trim yard lined with azalea shrubs. "Very quiet and settled."

The weight of his arm was pleasant. Megan allowed it to remain as they walked toward the garage. "I wouldn't think you'd find something quiet and settled terribly appealing."

"There's a time for porch swings and a time for roller coasters." Katch glanced down at her as she paused at the foot of the steps. "I'd think you'd know that."

"I do," she said, knowing her involvement with him was beginning to slip beyond her control. "I wasn't aware you did." Thoughtfully, Megan climbed the stairs. "It's rather a small-scale studio, I suppose, and not very impressive. It's really just a place to work where I won't disturb Pop and he won't disturb me."

Megan opened the door, flicking on the light as the sun was growing dim.

There was much less order here than she permitted herself in other areas of her life. The room was hers, personally, more exclusively than her bedroom in the house next door. There were tools—calipers, chisels, gouges, and an assortment of knives and files. There was the smock she'd carelessly thrown over a chair when Katch had called her downstairs. Future projects sat waiting inside, untouched slabs of limestone and chunks of wood. There was a precious piece of marble she hoarded like a miser. Everywhere, on shelves, tables and even the floor, were samples of her work.

Katch moved past her into the room. Strangely, Megan felt a flutter of nerves. She found herself wondering how to react if he spoke critically, or worse, offered some trite compliment. Her work was important to her and very personal. To her surprise she realized that she cared about his opinion. Quietly, she closed the door behind her, then stood with her back against it.

Katch had gone directly to a small walnut study of a young girl building a sand castle. She was particularly pleased with the piece, as she had achieved exactly the mood she had sought. There was more than youth and innocence in the child's face. The girl saw herself as the princess in the castle tower. The half-smile on her face made the onlooker believe in happy endings.

It was painstakingly detailed, the beginnings of a crenellated roof and the turrets of the castle, the slender fingers of the girl as she sculpted the sand. Her hair was long, falling over her shoulders and wisping into her face as though a breeze teased it. Megan had felt successful when the study had been complete, but now, watching Katch turn it over in his hands, his mouth oddly grave, his eyes intent, she felt a twinge of doubt.

"This is your work?" Because the silence had seemed so permanent, Megan jerked when Katch spoke.

"Well, yes." While she was still searching for something more to say, Katch turned away to prowl the room.

He picked up piece after piece, examining, saying nothing. As the silence dragged on, minute upon minute, Megan became more and more tense. If he'd just say something, she thought. She picked up the discarded smock and folded it, nervously smoothing creases as she listened to the soft sound of his tennis shoes on the wood floor.

"What are you doing here?"

She whirled, eyes wide. Whatever reaction she had expected, it certainly hadn't been anger. And there was anger on his face, a sharp, penetrating anger which caused her to grip the worn material of the smock tighter.

"I don't know what you mean." Megan's voice was calm, but her heart had begun to beat faster.

"Why are you hiding?" he demanded. "What are you afraid of?"

She shook her head in bewilderment. "I'm not hiding, Katch. You're not making any sense."

"I'm not making sense?" He took a step

toward her, then stopped, turning away to pace again. She watched in fascination. "Do you think it makes sense to create things like this and lock them up in a room over a garage?" He lifted polished limestone which had been formed into a head-and-shoulders study of a man and a woman in each other's arms. "When you've been given talent like this, you have an obligation. What are you going to do, continue to stack them in here until there isn't any more room?"

His reaction had thrown Megan completely off-balance. She looked around the room. "No, I…I take pieces into an art gallery downtown now and then. They sell fairly well, especially during the season, and—"

Katch's pungent oath cut her off. Megan gave her full attention back to him. Was this furious, disapproving man the same one who had amiably prepared trout in her kitchen a short time ago?

"I don't understand why you're so mad." Annoyed with herself for nervously pleating the material of the smock, Megan tossed it down.

"Waste," he said tersely, placing the

limestone back on the shelf. ''Waste infuriates me.'' He came to her, taking her deliberately by the shoulders. ''Why haven't you done anything with your work?'' His eyes were direct on hers, demanding answers, not evasions.

''It's not as simple as that,'' she began. ''I have responsibilities.''

''Your responsibilities are to yourself, to your talent.''

''You make it sound as though I've done something wrong.'' Confused, Megan searched his face. ''I've done what I know how to do. I don't understand why you're angry. There are things, like time and money, to be considered,'' she went on. ''A business to run. And reality to face.'' Megan shook her head. ''I can hardly cart my work to a Charleston art gallery and demand a showing.''

''That would make more sense than cloistering it up here.'' He released her abruptly, then paced again.

He was, Megan discovered, much more volatile than her first impression had allowed. She glanced at the clay wrapped in the damp towel. Her fingertips itched to work while fresh impressions were streaming through her brain.

"When's the last time you've been to New York?" Katch demanded, facing her again. "Chicago, L.A.?"

"We can't all be globetrotters," she told him. "Some are born to other things."

He picked up the sand-castle girl again, then strode over to the limestone couple. "I want these two," he stated. "Will you sell them to me?"

They were two of her favorites, though totally opposite in tone. "Yes, I suppose. If you want them."

"I'll give you five hundred." Megan's eyes widened. "Apiece."

"Oh, no, they're not worth—"

"They're worth a lot more, I imagine." Katch lifted the limestone. "Have you got a box I can carry them in?"

"Yes, but, Katch." Megan paused and pushed the bangs from her eyes. "A thousand dollars?"

He set down both pieces and came back to her. He was still angry; she could feel it vibrating from him. "Do you think it's safer to underestimate yourself than to face up to your own worth?''

Megan started to make a furious denial, then stopped. Uncertain, she made a helpless gesture with her hands. Katch turned away again to search for a box himself. She watched him as he wrapped the sculptures in old newspapers. The frown was still on his face, the temper in his eyes.

''I'll bring you a check,'' he stated, and was gone without another word.

Chapter 5

There was a long, high-pitched scream. The roller coaster rumbled along the track as it whipped around another curve and tilted its passengers. Lights along the midway were twinkling, and there was noise. Such noise. There was the whirl and whine of machinery, the electronic buzz and beeps from video games, the pop of arcade rifles and the call of concessionaires.

Tinny music floated all over, but for the most part, there was the sound of people. They were laughing, calling, talking, shouting. There were smells: popcorn, peanuts, grilled hot dogs, machine oil.

Megan loaded another clip into the scaled-down rifle and handed it to a would-be Wyatt Earp. "Rabbits are five points, ducks ten, deer twenty-five and the bears fifty."

The sixteen-year-old sharpshooter aimed and managed to bag a duck and a rabbit. He chose a rubber snake as his prize, to the ensuing screams and disgust of his girl.

Shaking her head, Megan watched them walk away. The boy slipped his arm around the girl's shoulders, then pursued the romance by dangling the snake in front of her face. He earned a quick jab in the ribs.

The crowd was thin tonight, but that was to be expected in the off-season. Particularly, Megan knew, when there were so many other parks with more rides, live entertainment and a more sophisticated selection of video games. She didn't mind the slack. Megan was preoccupied, as she had been since the evening Katch had seen her studio. In three days, she hadn't heard a word from him. At first, she had wanted badly to see him, to talk about the things he'd said to her. He had made her think, made her consider a part of herself she had ignored or submerged most of her life.

Her desire to speak with Katch had faded as the days had passed, however. After all, what right did he have to criticize her lifestyle? What right did he have to make her feel as if she'd committed a crime? He'd accused, tried and condemned her in the space of minutes. Then, he'd disappeared.

Three days, Megan mused, handing another hopeful deadeye a rifle. Three days without a word. And she'd watched for him—much to her self-disgust. She'd waited for him. As the days had passed, Megan had taken refuge in anger. Not only had he criticized and scolded her, she remembered, but he'd walked out with two of her favorite sculptures. A thousand dollars my foot, she mused, frowning fiercely as she slid a fresh clip into an empty rifle. Just talk, that's all. Talk. He does that very well. It was probably all a line, owning that restaurant. *But why?* Men like that don't need logical reasons, she decided. It's all ego.

''Men,'' she muttered as she handed a rifle to a new customer.

''I know what you mean, honey.'' The

plump blond woman took the rifle from Megan with a wink.

Megan pushed her bangs back and frowned deeper. "Who needs them?" she demanded.

The woman shouldered the rifle. "We do, honey. That's the problem."

Megan let out a long sigh as the woman earned 125 points. "Nice shooting," she congratulated. "Your choice on the second row."

"Let me have the hippo, sweetie. It looks a little like my second husband."

Laughing, Megan plucked it from the shelf and handed it over. "Here you go." With another wink, the woman tucked the hippo under her arm and waddled off.

Megan settled back while two kids tried their luck. The exchange had been typical of the informality enjoyed by people in amusement parks. She smiled, feeling less grim, if not entirely mollified by the woman's remarks. But she doesn't know Katch, Megan reflected, again exchanging a rifle for a quarter. And neither, she reminded herself, do I.

Automatically, Megan made change when a dollar bill was placed on the counter. "Ten shots for a quarter,'' she began the spiel. ''Rabbits are five, ducks ten...'' Megan pushed three quarters back as she reached for a rifle. The moment the fingers pushed the change back to her, she recognized them.

''I'll take a dollar's worth,'' Katch told her as she looked up in surprise. He grinned, then leaned over to press a quick kiss to her lips. ''For luck,'' he claimed when she jerked away.

Before Megan had pocketed the quarters, Katch had bull's-eyed every one of the bears.

''Wow!'' The two boys standing next to Katch were suitably impressed. ''Hey, mister, can you do it again?'' one asked.

''Maybe.'' Katch turned to Megan. ''Let's have a reload.'' Without speaking, she handed him the rifle.

''I like the perfume you're wearing,'' he commented as he sighed. ''What is it?''

''Gun oil.''

He laughed, then blasted the hapless bears one by one. The two boys gave simultaneous yelps of appreciation. A crowd began to gather.

''Hey, Megan.'' She glanced up to see the

Bailey twins leaning over the counter. Both pairs of eyes drifted meaningfully to Katch. "Isn't he the..."

"Yes," Megan said shortly, not wanting to explain.

"Delicious," Teri decided quietly, giving Katch a flirtatious smile when he straightened.

"Mmm-hmm," Jeri agreed with a twin smile.

Katch gave them a long, appreciative look.

"Here." Megan shoved the rifle at him. "This is your last quarter."

Katch accepted the rifle. "Thanks." He hefted it again. "Going to wish me luck?"

Megan met his eyes levelly. "Why not?"

"Meg, I'm crazy about you."

She dealt with the surge his careless words brought her as he picked off his fourth set of bears. Bystanders broke into raucous applause. Katch set the rifle on the counter, then gave his full attention to Meg.

"What'd I win?"

"Anything you want."

His grin was a flash, and his eyes never left her face. She blushed instantly, hating herself. Deliberately, she stepped to the side and gestured toward the prizes.

"I'll take Henry," he told her. When she gave him a puzzled look, he pointed. "The elephant." Glancing up, Megan spotted the three-foot lavender elephant. She lifted it down from its perch. Even as she set it on the counter for him, Katch took her hands. "And you."

She made her voice prim. "Only the items on display are eligible prizes."

"I love it when you talk that way," he commented.

"Stop it!" she hissed, flushing as she heard the Bailey twins giggle.

"We had a bet, remember?" Katch smiled at her. "It's Friday night."

Megan tried to tug her hands away, but his fingers interlocked with hers. "Who says I lost the bet?" she demanded. The crowd was still milling around the stand so she spoke in an undertone, but Katch didn't bother.

"Come on, Meg, I won fair and square. You're not going to welch, are you?"

"Shh!" She glanced behind him at the curious crowd. "I never welch," she whispered furiously. "And even if I did lose, which I never said I did, I can't leave the stand. I'm sure you can find somebody else to keep you company."

"I want you."

She struggled to keep her eyes steady on his. "Well, I can't leave. Someone has to run the booth."

"Megan." One of the part-timers slipped under the counter. "Pop sent me to relieve you." He smiled innocently when she gave him a disgusted look.

"Perfect timing," she mumbled, then stripped off the change apron and stuffed it in his hands. "Thanks a lot."

"Sure, Megan."

"Hey, keep this back there for me, will you?" Katch dumped the elephant into his arms and captured Megan's hands again as she ducked under the counter. As she straightened, he tugged, tumbling her into his arms.

The kiss was long and demanding. When Katch drew her away, her arms were around his neck. She left them there, staring up into his face with eyes newly aware and darkened.

"I've wanted to do that for three days," he murmured, and rubbed her nose lightly with his.

"Why didn't you?"

He lifted a brow at that, then grinned when her blush betrayed the impetuousness of her words.

"I didn't mean that the way it sounded," Megan began, dropping her arms and trying to wriggle away.

"Yes you did," he countered. Katch released her but dropped a friendly arm over her shoulder. "It was nice, don't spoil it." He took a sweeping glance of the park. "How about a tour?"

"I don't know why you want one. We're not selling."

"We'll see about that," he said, as maddeningly confident as ever. "But in any case, I'm interested. Do you know why people come here? To a place like this?" He gestured with his free arm to encompass the park.

"To be entertained," Megan told him as she followed the movement of his arm.

"You left out two of the most important

reasons,'' he added. ''To fantasize and to show off.''

They stopped to watch a middle-aged man strip out of his jacket and attempt to ring the bell. The hammer came down with a loud thump, but the ball rose only halfway up the pole. He rubbed his hands together and prepared to try again.

''Yes, you're right.'' Megan tossed her hair back with a move of her head, then smiled at Katch. ''You ought to know.''

He tilted his head and shot her a grin. ''Want me to ring the bell?''

''Muscles don't impress me,'' she said firmly.

''No?'' He guided her away with his arm still around her. ''What does?''

''Poetry,'' Megan decided all at once.

''Hmm.'' Katch rubbed his chin and avoided a trio of teenagers. ''How about a limerick? I know some great limericks.''

''I bet you do.'' Megan shook her head. ''I think I'll pass.''

''Coward.''

''Oh? Let's ride the roller coaster, then we'll see who's a coward.''

''You're on.'' Taking her hand, he set off

in a sprint. He stopped at the ticket booth, and gratefully she caught her breath.

I might as well face it, she reflected as she studied his face. I enjoy him. There isn't any use in pretending I don't.

"What are you thinking?" Katch demanded as he paid for their ride.

"That I could learn to like you—in three or four years. For short periods of time," she added, still smiling.

Katch took both her hands and kissed them, surprising Megan with the shock that raced up her arms. "Flatterer," he murmured, and his eyes laughed at her over their joined hands.

Distressed by the power she felt rushing through her system, Megan tried to tug her hands from his. It was imperative, for reasons only half-formed in her brain, that she keep their relationship casual.

"You have to hold my hand." Katch jerked his head toward the roller coaster. "I'm afraid of heights."

Megan laughed. She let herself forget the tempestuous instant and the hint of danger. She kept her hand in his.

Katch wasn't satisfied with only the roller

coaster. He pulled Megan to ride after ride. They were scrambled on the Mind Maze, spooked in the Haunted Castle and spun lazily on the Ferris wheel.

From the top of the wheel, they watched the colored lights of the park, and the sea stretching out to the right. The wind tossed her hair into her face. Katch took it in his hand as they rose toward the top again. When he kissed her, it felt natural and right…a shared thing, a moment which belonged only to them. The noise and people below were of another world. Theirs was only the gentle movement of the wheel and the dance of the breeze. And the touch of mouth on mouth. There was no demand, only an offering of pleasure.

Megan relaxed against him, finding her head fit naturally in the curve of his shoulder. Held close beside him, she watched the world revolve. Above, the stars were scattered and few. A waning moon shifted in and out of the clouds. The air was cool with a hint of the sea. She sighed, utterly content.

"When's the last time you did this?"

"Did what?" Megan tilted her head to

look at him. Their faces were close, but she felt no danger now, only satisfaction.

"Enjoyed this park." Katch had caught the confusion on her face. "Just enjoyed it, Megan, for the fun."

"I..." The Ferris wheel slowed, then stopped. The carts rocked gently as old passengers were exchanged for new. She remembered times when she had been very young. When had they stopped? "I don't know." Megan rose when the attendant lifted the safety bar.

This time, as she walked with Katch, she looked around thoughtfully. She saw several people she knew; locals out for an evening's entertainment mixed with tourists taking a preseason vacation.

"You need to do this more often," Katch commented, steering her toward the east end of the park. "Laugh," he continued as she turned her head to him. "Unbend, relax those restrictions you put on yourself."

Megan's spine stiffened. "For somebody who barely knows me, you seem remarkably certain of what's good for me."

"It isn't difficult." He stopped at a concession wagon and ordered two ice-cream cones. "You haven't any mysteries, Meg."

"Thank you very much."

With a laugh, Katch handed her a cone. "Don't get huffy, I meant that as a compliment."

"I suppose you've known a lot of sophisticated women."

Katch smiled, then his arm came around her as they began to walk again. "There's one, her name's Jessica. She's one of the most beautiful women I know."

"Really?" Megan licked at the soft swirl of vanilla.

"That blond, classical look. You know, fair skin, finely chiseled features, blue eyes. Terrific blue eyes."

"How interesting."

"Oh, she's all of that," he continued. "And more: intelligent, a sense of humor."

"You sound very fond of her." Megan gave the ice cream her undivided attention.

"A bit more than that actually. Jessica and I lived together for a number of years." He dropped the bomb matter-of-factly. "She's married now and has a couple of kids, but we still manage to see each other now and again. Maybe she can make it down for a few days, then you can meet her."

"Oh, really!" Megan stopped, incensed. "Flaunt your relationship somewhere else. If you think I want to meet your—your..."

"Sister," Katch supplied, then crunched into his cone. "You'd like her. Your ice cream's dripping, Meg."

They walked to the entrance gates of the park.

"It's a very nice park," Katch murmured. "Small but well set up. No bored-faced attendants." He reached absently in his pocket and pulled out a slip of paper.

"I forgot to give you your check."

Megan stuffed it into her pocket without even glancing at it. Her eyes were on Katch's face. She was all too aware of the direction his thoughts had taken. "My grandfather's devoted his life to this park," she reminded him.

"So have you," Katch said.

"Why do you want to buy it?" she asked. "To make money?"

Katch was silent for a long moment. By mutual consent, they cut across the boardwalk and moved down the sloping sand toward the water. "Is that such a bad reason, Megan? Do you object to making money?"

"No, of course not. That would be ridiculous."

"I wondered if that was why you haven't done anything with your sculpting."

"No. I do what I'm capable of doing, and what I have time for. There are priorities."

"Perhaps you have them wrong." Before she could comment, he spoke again. "How would it affect the park's business if it had some updated rides and an expanded arcade?"

"We can't afford..."

"That wasn't my question." He took her by the shoulders and his eyes were serious.

"Business would improve, naturally," Megan answered. "People come here to be entertained. The more entertainment provided, the slicker, the faster the entertainment, the happier they are. And the more money they spend."

Katch nodded as he searched her face. "Those were my thoughts."

"It's academic because we simply haven't the sort of money necessary for an overhaul."

"Hmm?" Though he was looking directly at her, Megan saw that his attention had wandered. She watched it refocus.

"What are you thinking?" she demanded.

The grip on her shoulder altered to a caress. "That you're extraordinarily beautiful."

Megan pulled away. "No, you weren't."

"It's what I'm thinking now." The gleam was back in his eyes as he put his hands to her waist. "It's what I was thinking the first time I saw you."

"You're ridiculous." She made an attempt to pull away, but he caught her closer.

"I've never denied that. But you can't call me ridiculous for finding you beautiful." The wind blew her hair back, leaving her face unframed. He laid a soft, unexpected kiss on her forehead. Megan felt her knees turn to water. She placed her hands on his chest both for support and in protest. "You're an artist." He drew her fractionally closer, and his voice lowered. "You recognize beauty when you see it."

"Don't!" The protest was feeble as she made no attempt to struggle out of his gentle hold.

‘‘Don’t what? Don’t kiss you?’’ Slowly, luxuriously, his mouth journeyed over her skin. ‘‘But I have to, Meg.’’ His lips touched hers softly, then withdrew, and her heart seemed to stop. The flavor of his lips as they brushed against hers overwhelmed her. They tempted, then ruled. With a moan of pleasure, Megan drew him close against her.

Something seemed to explode inside her as the kiss deepened. She clung to him a moment, dazed, then terrified by the power of it. Needs, emotions and new sensations tumbled together too quickly for her to control them. As panic swamped her, Megan struggled in his arms. She would have run, blindly, without direction, but Katch took her arms and held her still.

‘‘What is it? You’re trembling.’’ Gently, he tilted her chin until their eyes met. Hers were wide, his serious. ‘‘I didn’t mean to frighten you. I’m sorry.’’

The gentleness was nearly her undoing. Love, so newly discovered, hammered for release. She shook her head, knowing her voice would be thick with tears if she spoke. Swallowing, Megan prayed she could steady it.

"No, it's...I have to get back. They're closing." Behind him, she could see the lights flickering off.

"Meg." The tone halted her. It was not a demand this time, but a request. "Have dinner with me."

"No—"

"I haven't even suggested an evening," he pointed out mildly. "How about Monday?"

Megan stood firm. "No."

"Please."

Her resolution dissolved on a sigh. "You don't play fair," she murmured.

"Never. How about seven?"

"No picnics on the beach," she compromised.

"We'll eat inside, I promise."

"All right, but just dinner." She stepped away from him. "Now, I have to go."

"I'll walk you back." Katch took her hand and kissed it before she could stop him. "I have to get my elephant."

Chapter 6

Megan held Katch's face in her hands. With totally focused absorption, she formed his cheekbones. She had thought when she had first begun to work on this bust that morning that it would be good therapy. To an extent, she'd been right. The hours had passed peacefully, without the restless worry of the past two nights. Her mind was centered on her work, leaving no spaces for the disturbing thoughts that had plagued her all weekend.

She opened and closed her hands slowly, using the muscles until the cramping was a dull ache. A glance at her watch told her she had worked for longer than she'd intended. Late afternoon sun poured through the windows. Critically, as she pulled on each finger to soothe it, Megan studied her work.

The model was good, she decided, with just the proper touches of roughness and intelligence she had aimed for. The mouth was strong and sensuous, the eyes perceptive and far too aware. The mobility of the face which Megan found fascinating could only be suggested. It was a face that urged one to trust against better judgment and common sense.

Narrowing her eyes, she studied the clay replica of Katch's face. There are certain men, she thought, who make a career out of women—winning them, making love to them, leaving them. There are other men who settle down and marry, raise families. How could she doubt what category Katch fell into?

Megan rose to wash her hands. Infatuation, she reflected. It's simply infatuation. He's different, and I can't deny he's exciting. I wouldn't be human if I weren't flattered that he's attracted to me. I've overreacted, that's all. She dried her hands on a towel and tried to convince herself. A person doesn't fall in love this quickly. And if they do, it's just a surface thing, nothing lasting. Megan's eyes were drawn to the clay model. Katch's smile seemed to mock all her sensible arguments. She hurled the towel to the floor.

"It can't happen this fast!" she told him furiously. "Not this way. Not to me." She swung away from his assured expression. "I won't let it."

It's only the park he wants, she reminded herself. Once he's finally convinced he can't have it, he'll go away. The ache was unexpected, and unwelcome. That's what I want, she thought. For him to go away and leave us alone. She tried not to remember the new frontiers she had glimpsed while being held in his arms.

With a brisk shake of her head, Megan pulled the tie from her hair so that it tumbled back to brush her shoulders. I'll start in wood tomorrow, she decided, and covered the clay model. Tonight, I'll simply enjoy a dinner date with an attractive man. It's that simple.

With a great deal more ease than she was feeling, Megan took off her work smock and left her studio.

"Hi, sweetheart." Pop pulled the truck into the driveway just as Megan reached the bottom step.

She noticed the weariness the moment he climbed from the cab. Knowing he hated fussing, she said nothing, but walked over and slipped an arm around his waist.

"Hi, yourself. You've been gone a long time."

"A problem or two at the park," he told her as they moved together toward the house.

That explained the weariness, Megan thought as she pushed open the back door. "What sort of problem?" Megan waited for him to settle himself at the kitchen table before she walked to the stove to brew tea.

"Repairs, Megan, just repairs. The coaster and the Octopus and a few of the smaller rides." He leaned back in his chair as Megan turned to face him.

"How bad?"

Pop sighed, knowing it was better to tell

her outright than to hedge. "Ten thousand, maybe fifteen."

Megan let out a long, steady breath. "Ten thousand dollars." She ran a hand under her bangs to rub her brow. There was no purpose in asking if he was sure. If he'd had any doubt, he'd have kept the matter to himself.

"Well, we can come up with five," she began, lumping the check she had just received from Katch into their savings. "We'll have to have a more exact amount so we can decide how big a loan we'll need."

"Banks take a dim view of lending great lumps of money to people my age," Pop murmured.

Because she saw he was tired and discouraged, she spoke briskly. "Don't be silly." She walked back to the stove to set on the kettle. "In any case, they'd be lending it to the park, wouldn't they?" She tried not to think of tight money and high interest rates.

"I'll go see a few people tomorrow," he promised, reaching for his pipe as if to indicate their business talk was over. "You're having dinner with Katch tonight?"

"Yes." Megan took out cups and saucers.

"Fine young man." He puffed pleasantly on his pipe. "I like him. Has style."

"He has style all right," she grumbled as the kettle began to sing. Carefully, she poured boiling water into cups.

"Knows how to fish," Pop pointed out.

"Which, of course, makes him a paragon of virtue."

"Well, it doesn't make me think any less of him." He spoke genially, smiling into Megan's face. "I couldn't help noticing the two of you on the wheel the other night. You looked real pretty together."

"Pop, really." Feeling her cheeks warm, Megan walked back to fiddle with the dishes in the sink.

"You seemed to like him well enough then," he pointed out before he tested his tea. "I didn't notice any objections when he kissed you." Pop sipped, enjoying. "In fact, you seemed to like it."

"Pop!" Megan turned back, astonished.

"Now, Meg, I wasn't spying," he said soothingly, and coughed to mask a chuckle. "You were right out in public, you know.

I'd wager a lot of people noticed. Like I said, you looked real pretty together."

Megan came back to sit at the table without any idea of what she should say. "It was just a kiss," she managed at length. "It didn't mean anything."

Pop nodded twice and drank his tea.

"It didn't," Megan insisted.

He gave her one of his angelic smiles. "But you do like him, don't you?"

Megan dropped her eyes. "Sometimes," she murmured. "Sometimes I do."

Pop covered her hand with his and waited until she looked at him again. "Caring for someone is the easiest thing in the world if you let it be."

"I hardly know him," she said quickly.

"I trust him," Pop said simply.

Megan searched his face. "Why?"

After a shrug, Pop drew on his pipe again. "A feeling I have, a look in his eyes. In a people business like mine, you get to be a good judge of character. He has integrity. He wants his way, all right, but he doesn't cheat. That's important."

Megan sat silently for a moment, not

touching her cooling tea. "He wants the park," she said quietly.

Pop looked at her through a nimbus of pipe smoke. "Yes, I know. He said so up front. He doesn't sneak around either." Pop's expression softened a bit as he looked into Megan's eyes. "Things don't always stay the same in life, Megan. That's what makes it work."

"I don't know what you mean. Do you...are you thinking of selling him the park?"

Pop heard the underlying hint of panic and patted her hand again. "Let's not worry about that now. The first problem is getting the rides repaired for the Easter break. Why don't you wear the yellow dress I like tonight, Meg? The one with the little jacket. It makes me think of spring."

Megan considered questioning him further, then subsided. There was no harder nut to crack than her grandfather when he had made up his mind to close a subject. "All right. I think I'll go up and have a bath."

"Megan." She turned at the door and looked back at him. "Enjoy yourself. Sometimes it's best to roll with the punches."

When she walked away, he looked at the empty doorway and thoughtfully stroked his beard.

An hour later, Megan looked at herself in the yellow dress. The shade hinted at apricot and warmed against her skin. The lines were simple, suiting her willow-slim figure and height. Without the jacket, her arms and shoulders were bare but for wispy straps. She ran a brush through her hair in long, steady strokes. The tiny gold hoops in her ears were her only jewelry.

"Hey, Megan!"

The brush paused in midair as she watched her own eyes widen in the mirror. He wasn't really standing outside shouting for her!

"Meg!"

Shaking her head in disbelief, Megan went to the window. Katch stood two stories down. He lifted a hand in salute when she appeared in the window.

"What are you doing?" she demanded.

"Open the screen."

"Why?"

"Open it," he repeated.

"If you expect me to jump, you can forget

it.'' Out of curiosity, she leaned out the window.

''Catch!''

Her reflexes responded before she could think. Megan reached for the bundle he tossed up to her, and found her hands full of daffodils. She buried her face in the bouquet.

''They're beautiful.'' Her eyes smiled over the blooms and down at him. ''Thank you.''

''You're welcome,'' he returned. ''Are you coming down?''

''Yes.'' She tossed her hair behind her shoulder. ''Yes, yes, in a minute.''

Katch drove quickly and competently, but not toward Restaurant Row as Megan had anticipated. He turned toward the ocean and headed north. She relaxed, enjoying the quieting light of dusk and his effortless driving.

She recognized the area. The houses there were larger, more elaborate than those in and on the very outskirts of town. There were tall hedges to assure privacy both from other houses and the public beaches. There were neatly trimmed lawns, willows, blossoming crepe myrtle, and asphalt drives. Katch pulled into one set well away from the other homes and bordered by purplish shrubbery.

The house was small by the neighborhood standards, and done in the weathered wood Megan invariably found attractive. It was a split-level building, with an observation deck crowning the upper story.

"What's this?" she asked, liking the house immediately.

"This is where I live." Katch leaned across her to unlatch her door, then slid out his own side.

"You live here?"

Katch smiled at the surprised doubt in her voice. "I have to live somewhere, Meg."

She wandered farther along the stone path that led to the house. "I suppose I really didn't think about you buying a house here. It suggests roots."

"I have them," he told her. "I just transplant them easily."

She looked at the house, the widespread yard. "You've picked the perfect spot."

Katch took her hand, interlocking fingers. "Come inside," he invited.

"When did you buy this?" she asked as they climbed the front steps.

"Oh, a few months ago when I came through. I moved in last week and haven't had a lot of time to look for furniture." The key shot into the lock. "I've picked up a few things here and there, and had others sent down from my apartment in New York."

It was scantily furnished, but with style. There was a low, sectional sofa in biscuit with a hodgepodge of colored pillows and a wicker throne chair coupled with a large hanging ivy in a pottery dish. A pair of étagères in brass and glass held a collection of shells; on the oak planked floor lay a large sisal rug.

The room was open, with stairs to the right leading to the second level, and a stone fireplace on the left wall. The quick survey showed Megan he had not placed her sculptures in the main room. She wondered fleetingly what he had done with them.

"It's wonderful, Katch." She wandered to a window. The lawn sloped downward and ended in tall hedges that gave the house comfortable privacy. "Can you see the ocean from the top level?"

When he didn't answer, she turned back to him. Her smile faded against the intensity of his gaze. Her heart beat faster. This was the part of him she had to fear, not the amiable gallant who had tossed her daffodils.

She tilted her head back, afraid, but wanting to meet him equally. He brought his hands to her face, and she felt the hardness of his palms on her skin. He brushed her hair back from her face as he brought her closer. He lowered his mouth, pausing only briefly before it claimed hers, as if to ascertain the need mirrored in her eyes. The kiss was instantly deep, instantly seeking.

She had been a fool—a fool to believe she could talk herself out of being in love with him. A fool to think that reason had anything to do with the heart.

When Katch drew her away, Megan pressed her cheek against his chest, letting her arms wind their way around his waist. His hesitation was almost too brief to measure before he gathered her close. She felt his lips in her hair and sighed from the sheer joy of it. His heartbeat was quick and steady in her ear.

"Did you say something?" he murmured.

"Hmm? When?"

"Before." His fingers came up to massage the back of her neck. Megan shivered with pleasure as she tried to remember the world before she had been in his arms.

"I think I asked if I could see the ocean from the top level."

"Yes." Again he took his hands to her face to tilt it back for one long, searing kiss. "You can."

"Will you show me?"

The grip on her skin tightened and her eyes closed in anticipation of the next kiss. But he drew her away until only their hands were touching. "After dinner."

Megan, content with looking at him, smiled. "Are we eating here?"

"I hate restaurants," Katch said, leading her toward the kitchen.

"An odd sentiment from a man who owns one."

"Let's say there are times when I prefer more intimate surroundings."

"I see." He pushed open the door to the kitchen and Megan glanced around at efficiency in wood and stainless steel. "And who's doing the cooking this time?"

"We are," he said easily, and grinned at her. "How do you like your steak?"

There was a rich, red wine to accompany the meal they ate at a smoked-glass table. A dozen candles flickered on a sideboard behind them, held in small brass holders. Megan's mood was as mellow as the wine that waltzed in her head. The man across from her held her in the palm of his hand. When she rose to stack the dishes, he took her hand. "Not now. There's a moon tonight."

Without hesitation, she went with him.

They climbed the stairs together, wide, uncarpeted stairs which were split into two sections by a landing. He led her through the main bedroom, a room dominated by a large bed with brass head- and footboards. There were long glass doors which led to a walkway. From there, stairs ascended to the observation deck.

Megan could hear the breakers before she moved to the rail. Beyond the hedgerow, the surf was turbulent. White water frothed against the dark. The moon's light was thin, but was aided by the power of uncountable stars.

She took a long breath and leaned on the rail. "It's lovely here. I never tire of looking at the ocean." There was a click from his lighter, then tobacco mixed pleasantly with the scent of the sea.

"Do you ever think about traveling?"

Megan moved her shoulders, a sudden, restless gesture. "Of course, sometimes. It isn't possible right now."

Katch drew on the thin cigar. "Where would you go?"

"Where would I go?" she repeated.

"Yes, where would you go if you could?" The smoke from his cigar wafted upward and vanished. "Pretend, Meg. You like to pretend, don't you?"

She closed her eyes a moment, letting the wine swim with her thoughts. "New Orleans," she murmured. "I've always wanted to see New Orleans. And Paris. When I was young I used to dream about studying in Paris like the great artists." She opened her eyes again. "You've been there, I suppose. To New Orleans and to Paris?"

"Yes, I've been there."

"What are they like?"

Katch traced the line of her jaw with a

fingertip before answering. "New Orleans smells of the river and swelters in the summer. There's music at all hours from open nightclubs and street musicians. It moves constantly, like New York, but at a more civilized pace."

"And Paris?" Megan insisted, wanting to see her wishes through his eyes. "Tell me about Paris."

"It's ancient and elegant, like a grand old woman. It's not very clean, but it never seems to matter. It's best in the spring; nothing smells like Paris in the spring. I'd like to take you there." Unexpectedly he took her hair in his hand. His eyes were intense again and direct on hers. "I'd like to see the emotions you control break loose. You'd never restrict them in Paris."

"I don't do that." Something more than wine began to swim in her head.

He tossed the cigar over the rail, then his free hand came to her waist to press her body against his. "Don't you?" There was a hint of impatience in his voice as he began to slide the jacket from her shoulders. "You've passion, but you bank it down. It escapes into your work, but even that's kept closed up in a studio. When I kiss you, I can taste it struggling to the surface."

He freed her arms from the confines of the jacket and laid it over the rail. Slowly, deliberately, he ran his fingers over the naked skin, feeling the warmth of response. "One day it's going to break loose. I intend to be there when it does."

Katch pushed the straps from her shoulders and replaced them with his lips. Megan made no protest as the kisses trailed to her throat. His tongue played lightly with the pulse as his hand came up to cup her breast. But when his mouth came to hers, the gentleness fled, and with it her passivity. Hunger incited hunger.

When he nipped her bottom lip, she gasped with pleasure. His tongue was avid, searching while his hands began a quest of their own. He slipped the bodice of her dress to her waist, murmuring with approval as he found her naked breasts taut with desire. Megan allowed him his freedom, riding on the crest of the wave that rose inside her. She had no knowledge to guide her, no experience. Desire ruled and instinct followed.

She trailed her fingers along the back of

his neck, kneading the warm skin, thrilling to the response she felt to her touch. Here was a power she had never explored. She slipped her hands under the back of his sweater. Their journey was slow, exploring. She felt the muscles of his shoulders tense as her hands played over them.

The quality of the kiss changed from demanding to urgent. His passion swamped her, mixing with her own until the combined power was more than she could bear. The ache came from nowhere and spread through her with impossible rapidity. She hurt for him. Desire was a pain as sharp as it was irresistible. In surrender, in anticipation, Megan swayed against him.

"Katch." Her voice was husky. "I want to stay with you tonight."

She was crushed against him for a moment, held so tightly, so strongly, there was no room for breath. Then, slowly, she felt him loosen his hold. Taking her by the shoulders, Katch looked down at her, his eyes dark, spearing into hers. Her breath was uneven; shivers raced along her skin. Slowly, with hands that barely touched her skin, he slipped her dress back into place.

"I'll take you home now."

The shock of rejection struck her like a blow. Her mouth trembled open, then shut again. Quickly, fighting against the tears that were pressing for release, she fumbled for her jacket.

"Meg." He reached out to touch her shoulders, but she backed away.

"No. No, don't touch me." The tears were thickening her voice. She swallowed. "I won't be patted on the head. It appears I misunderstood."

"You didn't misunderstand anything," he tossed back. "And don't cry, damn it."

"I have no intention of crying," she said. "I'd like to go home." The hurt was in her eyes, shimmering behind the tears she denied.

"We'll talk." Katch took her hand, but she jerked it away.

"Oh, no. No, we won't." Megan straightened her shoulders and looked at him squarely. "We had dinner—things got a bit beyond what they should have. It's as simple as that, and it's over."

"It's not simple or over, Meg." Katch

took another long look into her eyes. ''But we'll drop it for now.''

Megan turned away and walked back down the stairs.

Chapter 7

Amusement parks lose their mystique in the light of day. Dirt, scratched paint and dents show up. What is shiny and bright under artificial light is ordinary in the sunshine. Only the very young or the very young hearted can believe in magic when faced with reality.

Megan knew her grandfather was perennially young. She loved him for it. Fondly, she watched him supervising repairs on the Haunted Castle. His ghosts, she thought with a smile, are important to him. She walked beside the track, avoiding her own ghost along the way. It had been ten days since Pop had told her of the repair problems. Ten days since she had seen Katch. Megan pushed thoughts of him from her mind and concentrated on her own reality—her grandfather and their park. She was old enough to know what was real and what was fantasy.

"Hi," she called out from behind him. "How are things going?"

Pop turned at the sound of her voice, and his grin was expansive. "Just fine, Megan." The sound of repairs echoed around his words. "Quicker than I thought they would. We'll be rolling before the Easter rush." He swung an arm around her shoulder and squeezed. "The smaller rides are already back in order. How about you?"

She made no objection when he began to steer her outside. The noise made it difficult to hear. "What about me?" she replied. The sudden flash of sunlight made her blink. The spring day had all the heat of midsummer.

"You've that unhappy look in your eyes. Have had, for more than a wcck." Pop rubbed his palm against her shoulder as if to warm her despite the strength of the sun.

''You know you don't hide things from me, Megan. I know you too well.''

She was silent a moment, wanting to choose her words carefully. ''I wasn't trying to hide anything, Pop.'' Megan shrugged, turning to watch the crew working on the roller coaster. ''It's just not important enough to talk about, that's all. How long before the coaster's fixed?''

''Important enough to make you unhappy,'' he countered, ignoring her evasion. ''That's plenty important to me. You haven't gotten too old to talk to me about your problems now, have you?''

She turned dark apologetic eyes on him. ''Oh no, Pop, I can always talk to you.''

''Well,'' he said simply, ''I'm listening.''

''I made a mistake, that's all.'' She shook her head and would have walked closer to inspect the work crew had he not held her to him with a firm hand.

''Megan.'' Pop placed both hands on her shoulders and looked into her eyes. As they were nearly the same height, their eyes were level. ''I'm going to ask you straight,'' he continued. ''Are you in love with him?''

''No,'' she denied quickly.

Pop raised an eyebrow. ‘‘I didn’t have to mention any names, I see.’’

Megan paused a moment. She had forgotten how shrewd her grandfather could be. ‘‘I thought I was,’’ she said more carefully. ‘‘I was wrong.’’

‘‘Then why are you so unhappy?’’

‘‘Pop, please.’’ She tried to back away, but again his broad hands held her steady.

‘‘You’ve always given me straight answers, Meg, even when I’ve had to drag them out of you.’’

She sighed, knowing evasions and half-truths were useless when he was in this mood. ‘‘All right. Yes, I’m in love with him, but it doesn’t matter.’’

‘‘Not a very bright statement from a bright girl like you,’’ he said with a gentle hint of disapproval. Megan shrugged. ‘‘Why don’t you explain why being in love doesn’t matter,’’ he invited.

‘‘Well, it certainly doesn’t work if you’re not loved back,’’ Megan murmured.

‘‘Who says you’re not?’’ Pop wanted to know. His voice was so indignant, she felt some of the ache subside.

‘‘Pop.’’ Her expression softened. ‘‘Just

because you love me doesn't mean everyone else does."

"What makes you so sure he doesn't?" her grandfather argued. "Did you ask him?"

"No!" Megan was so astonished, she nearly laughed at the thought.

"Why not? Things are simpler that way."

Megan took a deep breath, hoping to make him understand. "David Katcherton isn't a man who falls in love with a woman, not seriously. And certainly not with someone like me." The broad gesture she made was an attempt to enhance an explanation she knew was far from adequate. "He's been to Paris, he lives in New York. He has a sister named Jessica."

"That clears things up," Pop agreed, and Megan made a quick sound of frustration.

"I've never been anywhere." She dragged a hand through her hair. "In the summer I see millions, literally millions of people, but they're all transient. I don't know who they are. The only people I really know are ones who live right here. The farthest I've been away from the beach is Charleston."

Pop brushed a hand over her hair to

smooth it. "I've kept you too close," he murmured. "I always told myself there'd be other times."

"Oh no, Pop, I didn't mean it that way." She threw her arms around him, burying her face in his shoulder. "I didn't mean to sound that way. I love you, I love it here. I wouldn't change anything. That was hateful of me."

He laughed and patted her back. The subtle scent of her perfume reminded him forcefully that she was no longer a girl but a woman. The years had been incredibly quick. "You've never done a hateful thing in your life. We both know you've wanted to see a bit of the world, and I know you've stuck close to keep an eye on me. Oh yes," he said, anticipating her objection. "And I was selfish enough to let you."

"You've never done anything selfish," she retorted and drew away. "I only meant that Katch and I have so little common ground. He's bound to see things differently than I do. I'm out of my depth with him."

"You're a strong swimmer, as I recall." Pop shook his head at her expression and sighed. "All right, we'll let it lie awhile. You're also stubborn."

"Adamant," she corrected, smiling again. "It's a nicer word."

"Just a fancy way of saying pigheaded," Pop said bluntly, but his eyes smiled back at her. "Why aren't you back in your studio instead of hanging around an amusement park in the middle of the day?"

"It wasn't going very well," she confessed, thinking of the half-carved face that haunted her. "Besides, I've always had a thing for amusement parks." She tucked her arm in his as they began to walk again.

"Well, this one'll be in apple-pie order in another week," Pop said, looking around in satisfaction. "With luck, we'll have a good season and be able to pay back a healthy chunk of that ten thousand."

"Maybe the bank will send us some customers so they'll get their money faster," Megan suggested, half listening to the sound of hammer against wood as they drew closer to the roller coaster.

"Oh, I didn't get the money from the bank, I got it from—" Pop cut himself off abruptly. With a cough and a wheeze, he bent down to tie his shoe.

"You didn't get the money from the bank?" Megan frowned at the snowy white head in puzzlement. "Well, where in the world did you get it then?"

His answer was an unintelligible grunt.

"You don't know anybody with that kind of money," she began with a half-smile. "Where..." The smile flew away. "No. No, you didn't." Even as she denied it, Megan knew it had to be the truth. "You didn't get it from him?"

"Oh now, Megan, you weren't to know." Distress showed in his eyes and seemed to weaken his voice. "He especially didn't want you to know."

"Why?" she demanded. "Why did you do it?"

"It just sort of happened, Meg." Pop reached out to pat her hand in his old, soothing fashion. "He was here, I was telling him about the repairs and getting a loan, and he offered. It seemed like the perfect solution." He fiddled with his shoestrings. "Banks poke around and take all that time for paperwork, and he isn't charging me nearly as much interest. I thought you'd be happy about that..." He trailed off.

"Is everything in writing?" she asked, deadly calm.

"Of course." Pop assumed a vaguely injured air. "Katch said it didn't matter, but I know how fussy you are, so I had papers drawn up, nice and legal."

"Didn't matter," she repeated softly. "And what did you use as collateral?"

"The park, naturally."

"Naturally," she repeated. Fury bubbled in the single word. "I bet he loved that."

"Now, don't you worry, Megan. Everything's coming along just fine. The repairs are going well, and we'll be opening right on schedule. Besides," he added with a sigh, "you weren't even supposed to know. Katch wanted it that way."

"Oh, I'm sure he did," she said bitterly. "I'm sure he did."

Turning, she darted away. Pop watched her streak out of sight, then hauled himself to his feet. She had the devil's own temper when she cut loose, that girl. Brushing his hands together, he grinned. That, he decided, pleased with his own maneuvering, should stir up something.

Megan brought the bike to a halt at the crest of Katch's drive, then killed the engine. She took off her helmet and clipped it on the seat. He was not, she determined, going to get away with it.

Cutting across the lawn, she marched to the front door. The knock was closer to a pound but still brought no response. Megan stuffed her hands into her pockets and scowled. Her bike sat behind his black Porsche. Ignoring amenities, she tried the knob. When it turned, she didn't hesitate. She opened the door and walked inside.

The house was quiet. Instinct told her immediately that no one was inside. Still, she walked through the living room looking for signs of him.

A watch, wafer-thin and gold, was tossed on the glass shelves of the étagère. A Nikon camera sat on the coffee table, its back open and empty of film. A pair of disreputable tennis shoes were half under the couch. A volume of John Cheever lay beside them.

Abruptly, she realized what she had done.

She'd intruded where she had no right. She was both uncomfortable and fascinated. An ashtray held the short stub of a thin cigar. After a brief struggle with her conscience, she walked toward the kitchen. She wasn't prying, she told herself, only making certain he wasn't home. After all, his car was here and the door had been unlocked.

There was a cup in the sink and a half pot of cold coffee on the stove. He had spilled some on the counter and neglected to wipe it up. Megan curtailed the instinctive move to reach for a dish towel. As she turned to leave, a low mechanical hum from outside caught her attention. She walked to the window and saw him.

He was coming from the south side of the lawn, striding behind a power mower. He was naked to the waist, with jeans low and snug at his hips. He was tanned, a deep honey gold that glistened now with the effort of manual labor. She admired the play of muscles rippling down his arms and across his back.

Stepping back from the window with a jerk, she stormed through the side kitchen door and raced across the lawn.

The flurry of movement and a flash of crimson caught his eye. Katch glanced over as Megan moved toward him in a red tailored shirt and white jeans. Squinting against the sun, he wiped the back of his hand across his brow. He reached down and shut off the mower as she came to him.

"Hello, Meg," he said lightly, but his eyes weren't as casual.

"You have nerve, Katcherton," she began. "But even I didn't think you'd take advantage of a trusting old man."

He lifted a brow and leaned against the mower's handle. "Once more," he requested, "with clarity."

"You're the type who has to poke your fingers into other people's business," she continued. "You just had to be at the park, you just had to make a magnanimous offer with your tidy little pile of money."

"Ah, a glimmer of light." He stretched his back. "I didn't think you'd be thrilled the money came from me. It seems I was right."

"You knew I'd never allow it," she declared.

"I don't believe I considered that." He

leaned on the mower again, but there was nothing restful in the gesture. ‘‘You don’t run Pop’s life from what I’ve seen, Meg, and you certainly don’t run mine.’’

She did her best to keep her tone even. ‘‘I have a great deal of interest in the park and everything that pertains to it.’’

‘‘Fine, then you should be pleased that you have the money for the repairs quickly, and at a low rate of interest.’’ His tone was cool and businesslike.

‘‘Why?’’ she demanded. ‘‘Why did you lend us the money?’’

‘‘I don’t,’’ Katch said after a long, silent moment, ‘‘owe you any explanation.’’

‘‘Then I’ll give you one,’’ Megan tossed back. There was passion in her voice. ‘‘You saw an opportunity and grabbed it. I suppose that’s what people do in your sort of world. Take, without the least thought of the people involved.’’

‘‘Perhaps I’m confused.’’ His eyes were slate, opaque and unreadable. His voice matched them. ‘‘I was under the impression that I gave something.’’

‘‘*Lent* something,’’ Megan corrected. ‘‘With the park as collateral.’’

"If that's your problem, take it up with your grandfather." Katch bent down, reaching for the cord to restart the mower.

"You had no right to take advantage of him. He trusts everyone."

Katch released the cord again with a snap. "A shame it's not an inherited quality."

"I've no reason to trust you."

"And every reason, it appears, to mistrust me since the first moment." His eyes had narrowed as if in speculation. "Is it just me or a general antipathy to men?"

She refused to dignify the question with an answer. "You want the park," she began.

"Yes, and I made that clear from the beginning." Katch shoved the mower aside so that there was no obstacle between them. "I still intend to have it, but I don't need to be devious to get it. I still intend to have you." She stepped back but he was too quick. His fingers curled tightly around her upper arm. "Maybe I made a mistake by letting you go the other night."

"You didn't want me. It's just a game."

"Didn't want you?" She made another quick attempt to pull away and failed. "No, that's right, I didn't want you." He pulled her against him and her mouth was crushed and conquered. Her mind whirled with the shock of it. ''I don't want you now.'' Before she could speak, his mouth savaged hers again. There was a taste of brutality he had never shown her. ''Like I haven't wanted you for days.'' He pulled her to the ground.

''No,'' she said, frightened, ''don't.'' But his lips were silencing hers again.

There was none of the teasing persuasion he had shown her before, no light arrogance. These were primordial demands, eliciting primordial responses from her. He would take what he wanted, his way. He plundered, dragging her with him as he raced for more. Then his lips left hers, journeying to her throat before traveling downward. Megan felt she was suffocating, suffused with heat. Her breath caught in her lungs, emerging in quick gasps or moans. His fingers ran a bruising trail over her quivering flesh. He ran his thumb over the point of her breast, back and forth, until she was beyond fear, beyond thought. His mouth came back to hers, fever hot, desperate. She murmured mindlessly, clinging to him as her body shuddered with waves of need.

Katch lifted his head, and his breath was warm and erratic on her face. Megan's lids fluttered open, revealing eyes dazed with passion, heavy with desire. Silently, she trembled. If words had been hers, she would have told him that she loved him. There was no pride in her, no shame, only soaring need and a love that was painful in its strength.

"This isn't the place for you." His voice was rough as he rolled over on his back. They lay there a moment, side by side, without touching. "And this isn't the way."

Her mind was fogged, and her blood surging. "Katch," Megan managed his name and struggled to sit up. His eyes lingered on her form, then slid up slowly to brood on her face. It was flushed and aware. She wanted to touch him but was afraid.

For a moment their eyes met. "Did I hurt you?"

She shook her head in denial. Her body ached with longing.

"Go home then." He rose, giving her a last, brief glance. "Before I do." He turned and left her.

Megan heard the slam of the kitchen door.

Chapter 8

It was difficult for Megan to cope with the two-week influx of tourists and sun seekers. They came, as they did every Easter, in droves. It was a preview of what the summer would hold. They came to bake on the beach and impress those left at home with a spring tan. They came to be battered and bounced around by the waves. They came to have fun. And what better place to find it than on white sand beaches or in an ocean with a gentle undertow and cresting waves? They came to laugh and sought their entertainment on spiraling water slides, in noisy arcades or crowded amusement parks.

For the first time in her life, Megan found herself resenting the intrusion. She wanted the quiet, the solitude that went with a resort town in its off-season. She wanted to be alone, to work, to heal. It seemed her art was the only thing she could turn to for true comfort. She was unwilling to speak of her feelings to her grandfather. There was still too much to be sorted out in her own mind. Knowing her, and her need for privacy, Pop didn't question.

The hours she spent at the park were passed mechanically. The faces she saw were all strangers. Megan resented it. She resented their enjoyment when her own life was in such turmoil. She found solace in her studio. If the light in her studio burned long past midnight, she never noticed the time. Her energy was boundless, a nervous, trembling energy that kept her going.

It was afternoon at the amusement park. At the kiddie cars Megan was taking tickets and doing her best to keep the more aggressive youngsters from trampling others. Each time the fire engines, race cars, police cruisers and ambulances were loaded, she pushed the lever which sent the caravan around in its clanging, roaring circle. Children grinned fiercely and gripped steering wheels.

One toddler rode as fire chief with eyes wide with stunned pleasure. Even though she'd been on duty nearly four hours, Megan smiled.

"Excuse me." Megan glanced over at the voice, prepared to answer a parental question. The woman was an exquisite blonde, with a mane of hair tied back from a delicately molded face. "You're Megan, aren't you? Megan Miller?"

"Yes. May I help you?"

"I'm Jessica Delaney."

Megan wondered that she hadn't seen it instantly. "Katch's sister."

"Yes." Jessica smiled. "How clever of you—but Katch told me you were. There is a family resemblance, of course, but so few people notice it unless we're standing together."

Megan's artist eyes could see the similar bone structure beneath the surface differences. Jessica's eyes were blue, as Katch had said, and the brows above them more delicate than his, but there were the same thick lashes and long lids.

"I'm glad to meet you." Megan reached for something to say. "Are you visiting Katch?" She didn't look like a woman who would patronize amusement parks, more likely country clubs or theaters.

"For a day or so." Jessica gestured to the adjoining ride where children flew miniature piper cubs in the inevitable circle. "My family's with me. Rob, my husband." Megan smiled at a tall man with a straight shock of dark hair and an attractive, angular face. "And my girls, Erin and Laura." She nodded to the two caramel-haired girls of approximately four and six riding double in a plane.

"They're beautiful."

"We like them," Jessica said comfortably. "Katch didn't know where I might find you in the park, but he described you very accurately."

"Is he here?" Megan asked, trying without much success to sound offhanded even as her eyes scanned the crowd.

"No, he had some business to attend to."

The timer rang, signaling the ride's end. "Excuse me a moment," Megan murmured. Grateful for the interruption, she supervised the unloading and loading of children. It gave her the time she needed to steady herself. Her two final customers were Katch's nieces. Erin, the elder, smiled at her with eyes the identical shade of her uncle's.

"I'm driving," she said positively as her sister settled beside her. "She only rides."

"I do not." Laura gripped the twin steering wheel passionately.

"It runs in the family," Jessica stated from behind her. "Stubbornness." Megan hooked the last safety belt and returned to the controls. "You've probably noticed it."

Megan smiled at her. "Yes, once or twice." The lights and noise spun and circled behind her.

"I know you're busy," Jessica stated, glancing at the packed vehicles.

Megan gave a small shrug as she followed her gaze. "It's mostly a matter of making certain everyone stays strapped in and no one's unhappy."

"My little angels," Jessica said, "will insist on dashing off to the next adventure the moment the ride's over.'' She paused. ''Could we talk after you're finished here?''

Megan frowned. ''Well, yes, I suppose...I'm due relief in an hour.''

''Wonderful.'' Jessica's smile was as charming as her brother's. ''I'd like to go to your studio, if that suits you. I could meet you in an hour and a half.''

''At my studio?''

''Wonderful!'' Jessica said again and patted Megan's hand. ''Katch gave me directions.''

The timer rang again, recalling Megan to duty. As she started yet another round of junior rides she wondered why Jessica had insisted on a date in her studio.

With a furrowed brow, Megan studied herself in the bedroom mirror. Would a man who admired Jessica's soft, delicate beauty be attracted to someone who seemed to be all planes and angles? Megan shrugged her shoulders as if it didn't matter. She twirled the stem of the brush idly between her fingers. She supposed that he, like the majority of people who came here, was looking for some passing entertainment

"You are," she said softly to the woman in the glass, "such a fool." She closed her eyes, not wanting to see the reflected accusation. Because you can't let go, her mind continued ruthlessly. Because it doesn't really matter to you why he wanted you with him, just that he wanted you. And you wish, you wish with all your heart that he still did.

She shook her head, disturbing the work she had done with the brush. It was time to stop thinking of it. Jessica Delaney would be arriving any moment.

Why? Megan set down her brush and frowned into middle distance. Why was she coming? What could she possibly want? Megan still had no sensible answer. I haven't heard from Katch in two weeks, she reflected. Why should his sister suddenly want to see me?

The sound of a car pulling into the drive below interrupted her thoughts. Megan walked to the window in time to see Jessica get out of Katch's Porsche.

Megan reached the back stoop before Jessica, as she had been taking a long, leisurely look at the yard. ''Hello.'' Megan felt awkward and rustic. She hesitated briefly before stepping away from the door.

''What a lovely place.'' Jessica's smile was so like Katch's that Megan's heart lurched. ''How I wish my azaleas looked like yours.''

''Pop—my grandfather babies them.''

''Yes.'' The blue eyes were warm and personal. ''I've heard wonderful things about your grandfather. I'd love to meet him.''

''He's still at the park.'' Her sense of awkwardness was fading. Charm definitely ran in the Katcherton family. ''Would you like some coffee? Tea?''

''Maybe later. Let's go up to the studio, shall we?''

''If you don't mind my asking, Mrs. Delaney—''

''Jessica,'' she interrupted cheerfully and began to climb the open back stairs.

''Jessica,'' Megan agreed, ''how did you know I had a studio, and that it was over the garage?''

''Oh, Katch told me,'' Jessica said breezily. ''He tells me a great many things.'' She stood to the side of the door and waited for Megan to open it. "I'm very anxious to see your work. I dabble in oil from time to time."

"Do you?" Jessica's interest now made more sense. Artistic kinship.

"Badly, I'm afraid, which is a constant source of frustration to me." Again the Katcherton smile bloomed on her face.

Megan's reaction was unexpectedly sharp and swift. She fumbled for the doorknob. "I've never had much luck on canvas," she said quickly. She needed words, lots of words to cover what she feared was much too noticeable. "Nothing seems to come out the way I intend," she continued as they entered the studio. "It's maddening not to be able to express yourself properly. I do some airbrushing during the summer rush, but…"

Jessica wasn't listening. She moved around the room much the same way her brother had—intently, gracefully, silently. She fingered a piece here, lifted a piece there. Once, she studied a small ivory unicorn for so long, Megan fidgeted with nerves.

What was she doing? she wondered. *And why?*

Sunlight stippled the floor. Dust motes danced in the early evening light. Too late, Megan recalled the bust of Katch. One slanted beam of sun fell on it, highlighting the planes the chisel had already defined. Though it was still rough hewn and far from finished, it was unmistakably Katch. Feeling foolish, Megan walked over to stand in front of it, hoping to conceal it from Jessica's view.

"Katch was right," Jessica murmured. She still held the unicorn, stroking it with her fingertips. "He invariably is. Normally that annoys me to distraction, but not this time." The resemblance to Katch was startling now. Megan's fingers itched to make a quick sketch even as she tried to follow the twisting roads in Jessica's conversation.

"Right about what?"

"Your extraordinary talent."

"What?" Meg's eyes widened.

"Katch told me your work was remarkable," she went on, giving the unicorn a final study before setting it down. "I agreed when I received the two pieces he sent up to me, but they were only two, after all." She picked up a chisel and tapped it absently against her palm while her eyes continued to wander. "This is astonishing."

"He sent you the sculptures he bought from me?"

"Yes, a few weeks ago. I was very impressed." Jessica set down the chisel with a clatter and moved to a nearly completed study in limestone of a woman rising from the sea. It was the piece Megan had been working on before she had set it aside to begin Katch's bust. "This is fabulous!" Jessica declared. "I'm going to have to have it as well as the unicorn. The response to the two pieces Katch sent me has been very favorable."

"I don't understand what you're talking about." Try as she might, Megan couldn't keep up with Jessica's conversation. "Whose response?"

"My clients'," said Jessica. "At my gallery in New York." She gave Megan a brilliant smile. "Didn't I tell you I run my own gallery?"

"No," Megan answered. "No, you didn't."

"I suppose I thought Katch did. I'd better start at the beginning then."

"I'd really appreciate it if you would," Megan told her, and waited until she had settled herself in the small wooden chair beside her.

"Katch sent me two of your pieces a few weeks ago," Jessica began briskly. "He wanted a professional opinion. I may only be able to dabble in oil, but I know art." She spoke with a confidence that Megan recognized. "Since I knew I'd never make it as a working artist, I put all the years of study to good use. I opened a gallery in Manhattan. *Jessica's.* Over the past six years, I've developed a rather nice clientele." She smiled. "So naturally, when my wandering brother saw your work, he sent it off to me. He always has his instincts verified by an expert, then plunges along his own way notwithstanding." She sighed indulgently. "I happen to know he was advised against building that hospital in Central Africa last year but he did it anyway. He does what he wants to."

"Hospital." Megan barely made the jump to Jessica's new train of thought.

"Yes, a children's hospital. He has a soft spot for kids." Jessica tried to speak teasingly, but the love came through. "He did some astonishing things for orphaned refugees after Vietnam. And there was the really fabulous little park he built in New South Wales."

Megan sat dumbly. Could they possibly be speaking about the same David Katcherton? Was this the man who had brashly approached her in the local market?

She remembered with uncomfortable clarity that she had accused him of trying to cheat her grandfather. She had told herself that he was an opportunist, a man spoiled by wealth and good looks. She'd tried to tell herself he was irresponsible, undependable, a man in search of his own pleasure.

"I didn't know," she murmured. "I didn't know anything about it."

"Oh, Katch keeps a low profile when he chooses," Jessica told her. "And he chooses to have no publicity when he's doing that sort of thing. He has incredible energy and outrageous self-confidence, but he's also very warm." Her gaze slipped beyond

Megan's shoulder. "But then, you appear to know him well."

For a moment, Megan regarded Jessica blankly. Then she twisted her head and saw Katch's bust. In her confusion, she had forgotten her desire to conceal it. Slowly, she turned her head back, trying to keep her voice and face passive.

"No. No, really I don't think I know him at all. He has a fascinating face. I couldn't resist sculpting it."

She noted a glint of understanding in Jessica's eyes. "He's a fascinating man," Jessica murmured.

Megan's gaze faltered.

"I'm sorry," Jessica said immediately. "I've intruded, a bad habit of mine. We won't talk about Katch. Let's talk about your showing."

Megan lifted her eyes again. "My what?"

"Your showing," Jessica repeated, dashing swiftly up a new path. "When do you think you'll have enough pieces ready? You certainly have a tremendous start here, and Katch mentioned something about a gallery in town having some of your pieces. I think we can shoot for the fall."

"Please, Jessica, I don't know what you're talking about." A note of panic slipped into Megan's voice. It was faint, almost buried, but Jessica detected it. She reached over and took both of Megan's hands. The grip was surprisingly firm.

"Megan, you have something special, something powerful. It's time to share it." She rose then, urging Megan up with her. "Let's have that coffee now, shall we? And we'll talk about it."

An hour later, Megan sat alone in the kitchen. Darkness was encroaching, but she didn't rise from the table to switch on the light. Two cups sat, her own half-filled with now cold coffee, Jessica's empty but for dregs. She tried to take her mind methodically over what had happened in the last sixty minutes.

A showing at Jessica's, an art gallery in Manhattan. New York. A public show. Of her work.

It didn't happen, she thought. I imagined it. Then she looked down at the empty cup across from her. The air still smelled faintly of Jessica's light, sophisticated scent.

Half-dazed, Megan took both cups to the

sink and automatically began rinsing them. How did she talk me into it? she wondered. I was agreeing to dates and details before I had agreed to do the showing. Does anyone ever say no to a Katcherton? She sighed and looked down at her wet hands. I have to call him. The knowledge increased the sense of panic. *I have to.*

Carefully, she placed the washed cups and saucers in the drainboard. I have to thank him. Nerves fluttered in her throat, but she made a pretense, for herself, of casually drying her damp hands on the hips of her jeans. She walked to the wall phone beside the stove.

"It's simple," she whispered, then bit her lip. She cleared her throat. "All I have to do is thank him, that's all. It'll only take a minute." Megan reached for the phone, then drew her hand away. Her mind raced on with her heartbeat.

She lifted the receiver. She knew the number. Hadn't she started to dial it a dozen times during the past two weeks? She took a long breath before pushing the first digit. It would take five minutes, and then, in all probability, she'd have no reason to contact him again. It would be better if they erased the remnants of their last meeting. It would be easier if their relationship ended on a calmer, more civilized note. Megan pressed the last button and waited for the click of connection, the whisper of transmitters and the ring.

It took four rings—four long, endless rings before he picked up the phone.

"Katch." His name was barely audible. She closed her eyes.

"Meg?"

"Yes, I..." She fought herself to speak. "I hope I'm not calling you at a bad time." How trite, she thought desperately. How ordinary.

"Are you all right?" There was concern in the question.

"Yes, yes, of course." Her mind fretted for the simple, casual words she had planned to speak. "Katch, I wanted to talk to you. Your sister was here—"

"I know, she got back a few minutes ago." There was a trace of impatience in his tone. "Is anything wrong?"

"No, nothing's wrong." Her voice refused to level. Megan searched for a quick way to end the conversation.

"Are you alone?"

"Yes, I..."

"I'll be there in ten minutes."

"No." Megan ran a frustrated hand through her hair. "No, please—"

"Ten minutes," he repeated and broke the connection.

Chapter 9

Megan stared at the dead receiver for several silent moments. How had she, in a few uncompleted sentences, managed to make such a mess of things? She didn't want him to come. She never wanted to see him again. *That is a lie.*

Carefully, Megan replaced the receiver. I do want to see him, she admitted, have wanted to see him for days. It's just that I'm afraid to see him. Turning, she gazed blindly around the kitchen. The room was almost in complete darkness now. The table and chairs were dark shadows. She walked to the switch, avoiding obstacles with the knowledge of years. The room flooded with brightness. That's better, she thought, more secure in the artificial light. Coffee, she decided, needing something, anything, to occupy her hands. I'll make fresh coffee.

Megan went to the percolator and began a step-by-step preparation, but her nerves continued to jump. In a few moments, she hoped, she'd be calm again. When he arrived, she would say what she needed to say, and then they would part.

The phone rang, and she jolted, juggling the cup she held and nearly dropping it. Chiding herself, Megan set it down and answered the call.

"Hello, Megan." Pop's voice crackled jovially across the wire.

"Pop...are you still at the park?" What time is it? she wondered distractedly and glanced down at her watch.

"That's why I called. George stopped by. We're going to have dinner in town. I didn't want you to worry."

"I won't." She smiled as the band of tension around her head loosened. "I suppose you and George have a lot of fish stories to exchange.''

''His have gotten bigger since he retired,'' Pop claimed. ''Hey, why don't you run into town, sweetheart? We'll treat you.''

''You two just want an audience,'' she accused and her smile deepened with Pop's chuckle. ''But I'll pass tonight, thanks. As I recall, there's some leftover spaghetti in the fridge.''

''I'll bring you back dessert.'' It was an old custom. For as long as Megan could remember, if Pop had dinner without her, he'd bring her back some treat. ''What do you want?''

''Rainbow sherbet,'' she decided instantly. ''Have a good time.''

''I will, darling. Don't work too late.''

As she hung up the phone, Megan asked herself why she hadn't told her grandfather of Katch's impending visit. Why hadn't she mentioned Jessica or the incredible plans that had been made? It has to wait until we can talk, she told herself. Really talk. It's the only way I'll be certain how he really feels—and how everything will affect him.

It's probably a bad idea. Megan began to

fret, pushing a hand through her hair in agitation. It's a crazy idea. How can I go to New York and—

Her thoughts were interrupted by the glaring sweep of headlights against the kitchen window. She struggled to compose herself, going deliberately to the cupboard to close it before heading to the screen door.

Katch stepped onto the stoop as she reached for the handle. For a moment, in silence, they studied each other through the mesh. She heard the soft flutter of moths' wings on the outside light.

Finally he turned the knob and opened the door. After he had shut it quietly behind him, he reached up to touch her cheek. His hand lingered there while his eyes traveled her face.

"You sounded upset."

Megan moistened her lips. "No, no, I'm fine." She stepped back so that his palm no longer touched her skin. Slowly, his eyes on hers, Katch lowered his hand. "I'm sorry I bothered you—"

"Megan, stop it." His voice was quiet and controlled. Her eyes came back to his, a little puzzled, a little desperate. ''Stop backing away from me. Stop apologizing.''

Her hands fluttered once before she could control the movement. ''I'm making coffee,'' she began. ''It should be ready in a minute.'' She would have turned to arrange the cups and saucers, but he took her arm.

''I didn't come for coffee.'' His hand slid down until it encircled her wrist. Her pulse vibrated against his fingers.

''Katch, please, don't make this difficult.''

Something flared in his eyes while she watched. Then it was gone, and her hand was released. ''I'm sorry. I've had some difficulty the past couple of weeks dealing with what happened the last time I saw you.'' He noted the color that shot into her cheeks, but she kept her eyes steady. He slipped his hands into his pockets. ''Megan, I'd like to make it up to you.''

Megan shook her head, disturbed by the gentleness in his voice, and turned to the coffee pot.

''Don't you want to forgive me?''

The question had her turning back, her

eyes darkened with distressed confusion. "No...that is, yes, of course."

"Of course you don't want to forgive me?" There was a faint glimmer of a smile in his eyes and the charm was around his mouth. She could feel herself sinking.

"Yes, of course I forgive you," she corrected and this time did turn to the coffee. "It's forgotten." He laid his hands on her shoulders, and she jumped.

"Is it?" Katch turned her until they were again face-to-face. The glimpse of humor in his eyes was gone. "You can't seem to abide my touching you. I don't much like thinking I frighten you."

She made a conscious effort to relax under his hands. "You don't frighten me, Katch," Megan murmured. "You confuse me. Constantly."

She watched his brow lift in consideration. "I don't have any intention of confusing you. I am sorry, Megan."

"Yes." She smiled, recognizing the simple sincerity. "I know you are."

He drew her closer. "Can we kiss and make up then?"

Megan started to protest, but his mouth

was already on hers, light and gentle. Her heart began to hammer in her throat. He made no attempt to deepen the kiss. His hands were easy on her shoulders. Against all the warnings of her mind, she relaxed against him, inviting him to take whatever he chose. But he took no more.

Katch drew her away, waiting until her heavy lids fluttered open before he touched her hair. Without speaking, he turned and paced to the window. Megan struggled to fill the new gap.

"I wanted to talk to you about your sister." She busied her hands with the now noisy percolator. "Or, more accurately, about what Jessica came to see me about."

Katch turned his head, watching her pour the coffee into the waiting cups. He walked to the refrigerator and took out the milk.

"All right." Standing beside her now, he poured milk into one cup and, at her nod, into the second.

"Why didn't you tell me you were sending my work to your sister?"

"I thought it best to wait until I had her opinion." Katch sat beside Megan and cradled the cup in both hands. "I trust her...."

And I thought you'd trust her opinion more than mine. Are you going to do the showing? Jessica and I didn't have time to talk before you called.''

She shifted in her chair, studied her coffee, then looked directly at him. ''She's very persuasive. I was agreeing before I realized it.''

''Good,'' Katch said simply and drank.

''I want to thank you,'' Meg continued in a stronger voice, ''for arranging things.''

''I didn't arrange anything,'' he responded. ''Jessica makes her own decisions, personal and professional. I simply sent her your sculptures for an opinion.''

''Then I'll thank you for that, for making a move I might never have made for the hundreds of reasons which occurred to me five minutes after she'd left.''

Katch shrugged. ''All right, if you're determined to be grateful.''

''I am,'' she said. ''And I'm scared,'' she continued, ''really terrified at the thought of putting my work on public display.'' Megan let out a shaky breath at the admission. ''I may despise you when all this is over and art critics stomp all over my ego, so you'd better take the gratitude now."

Katch crossed to her, and her heart lifted dizzily, so sure was she that he would take her into his arms. He merely stroked her cheek with the back of his hand. "When you're a smashing success, you can give it to me again." He smiled at her, and the world snapped into sharp focus. Until that moment, she hadn't realized how dull everything had been without him.

"I'm so glad you came," she whispered and, unable to resist, slipped her arms around him, pressing her face into his shoulder. After a moment, he rested his hands lightly at her waist. "I'm sorry for the things I said…about the loan. I didn't mean any of it really, but I say horrible things when I lose my temper."

"Is this your turn to be penitent?"

He made her laugh. "Yes." She smiled and tilted back her head. Her arms stayed around him. He kissed her and drew away. Reluctantly, she let him slip out of her arms. Then he stood silently, staring down at her.

"What are you doing?" she asked with a quick, self-conscious smile.

"Memorizing your face. Have you eaten?"

She shook her head, wondering why it should come as a surprise that he continued to baffle her. "No, I was going to heat up some leftovers."

"Unacceptable. Want a pizza?"

"*Mmm,* I'd love it, but you have company."

"Jessica and Rob took the kids to play miniature golf. I won't be missed." Katch held out his hands. "Come on."

His eyes were smiling, and her heart was lost. "Oh wait," she began even as she put her hand into his. Quickly, Megan scrawled a message on the chalkboard by the screen door.

OUT WITH KATCH

It was enough.

Chapter 10

Katch drove along Ocean Boulevard so they could creep along in the traffic filled with tourists and beachers. Car radios were turned up high and windows rolled down low. Laughter and music poured out everywhere. The lights from a twin Ferris wheel glittered red and blue in the distance. People sat out on their hotel balconies, with colorful beach towels flapping over the railings, as they watched the sluggish flow of cars and pedestrians. To the left, there were glimpses of the sea in between buildings.

Sleepily content after pizza and Chianti,

Megan snuggled deeper into the soft leather seat. "Things'll quiet down after this weekend," she commented. "Until Memorial Day."

"Do you ever feel as though you're being invaded?" Katch asked her with a gesture at the clogged traffic.

"I like the crowds," she said immediately, then laughed. "And I like the winter when the beaches are deserted. I suppose there's something about the honky-tonk that appeals to me, especially since I know I'm going to have a few isolated months in the winter."

"That's your time," Katch murmured, glancing back at her. "The time you give yourself for sculpting."

She shrugged, a bit uncomfortable with the intense look. "I do some in the summer, too—when I can. Time's something I forgot when Jessica was talking about a showing and making all those plans..." Megan trailed off, frowning. "I don't know how I can possibly get things ready."

"Not backing out, are you?"

"No, but—" The look in his eyes had her

swallowing excuses. "No," she said more firmly. "I'm not backing out."

"What're you working on now?"

"I, ah..." Megan looked fixedly out the window, thinking of the half-formed bust of Katch's head. "It's just..." She shrugged and began to fiddle with the dial of the radio. "It's just a wood carving."

"Of what?"

Megan made a few inarticulate mumbles until Katch turned to grin at her. "A pirate," she decided as the light from a street lamp slanted over his face, throwing it into planes and shadows. "It's the head of a pirate."

His brow lifted at the sudden, narrow-eyed concentration with which she was studying him. "I'd like to see it."

"It's not finished," she said quickly. "I've barely got the clay model done. In any case, I might have to put it off if I'm going to get the rest of my pieces organized for your sister."

"Meg, why don't you stop worrying and just enjoy it?"

Confused, she shook her head and stared at him. "Enjoy it?"

"The show," he said, ruffling her hair.

"Oh, yes." She fought to get her thoughts back into some kind of order. "I will...after it's over," she added with a smile. "Do you think you'll be in New York, then?"

As the rhythm of the traffic picked up, he shifted into third. "I'm considering it."

"I'd like you to be there if you could arrange it." When he laughed, shaking his head, she continued, "It's just that I'm going to need all the friendly faces I can get."

"You're not going to need anything but your sculptures," Katch corrected, but the amusement was still in his eyes. "Don't you think I'd want to be around the night of your opening so that I can brag I discovered you?"

"Let's just hope we both don't live to regret it," Megan muttered, but he only laughed again. "You just can't consider the possibility that you might have made a mistake," she accused testily.

"You can't consider the possibility that you might be successful," he countered.

Megan opened her mouth, then shut it again. "Well," she said after a moment, "we're both right." Waiting until they were stopped in traffic again, Megan touched his shoulder. "Katch?"

"Hmm?"

"Why did you build a hospital in Central Africa?"

He turned to her then, a faint frown between his brows. "It was needed," he said simply.

"Just that?" she persisted, though she could see he wasn't pleased with her question. "I mean, Jessica said you were advised against it, and—"

"As it happens, I have a comfortable amount of money." He cut her off with an annoyed movement of his shoulder. "I do what I choose with it." Seeing her expression, Katch shook his head. "There are things I want to do, that's all. Don't canonize me, Meg."

She relaxed again and found herself brushing at the curls over his ear. "I wouldn't dream of it." He'd rather be thought of as eccentric than benevolent, she mused. And how much simpler it was to love him, knowing that one small secret. "You're much easier to like than I thought you'd be when you made a nuisance of yourself in the market.''

''I tried to tell you,'' he pointed out. ''You were too busy pretending you weren't interested.''

''I wasn't interested,'' Megan insisted, ''in the least.'' He turned to grin at her and she found herself laughing. ''Well, not very much anyway.'' When he swung the car onto a side street, she looked back at him in question. ''What are you doing?''

''Let's go out on the boardwalk.'' Expertly, he slid the Porsche into a parking space. ''Maybe I'll buy you a souvenir.'' He was already out of the car—primed, impatient.

''Oh, I love rash promises,'' Megan crowed as she joined him.

''I said maybe.''

''I didn't hear that part. And,'' she added as she laced her fingers with his, ''I want something extravagant.''

''Such as?'' They jaywalked, maneuvering around stopped cars.

''I'll know when I see it.''

The boardwalk was crowded, full of people and light and noise. The breeze off the ocean carried the scent of salt to compete with the aroma of grilling meat from concessions. Instead of going into one of the little shops, Katch pulled Megan into an arcade.

"Big talk about presents and no delivery," Megan said in disgust as Katch exchanged bills for tokens.

"It's early yet. Here." He poured a few tokens into her hand. "Why don't you try your luck at saving the galaxy from invaders?"

With a smirk, Megan chose a machine, then slipped two tokens into the slot. "I'll go first." Pressing the start button, she took the control stick in hand and began systematically to vaporize the enemy. Brows knit, she swung her ship right and left while the machine exploded with color and noise with each hit. Amused, Katch dipped his hands into his pockets and watched her face. It was a more interesting show than the sophisticated graphics.

She chewed her bottom lip while maneuvering into position, narrowing her eyes when a laser blast headed her way. Her breath hissed through her teeth at a narrow escape. But all the while, her face held that composed, almost serious expression that was so much a part of her. Fighting gamely to avoid being blown up in cross fire, Megan's ship at last succumbed.

"Well," Katch murmured, glancing at her score as she wiped her hands on the back of her jeans. "You're pretty good."

"You have to be," Megan returned soberly, "when you're the planet's last hope."

With a chuckle, he nudged her out of the way and took the control.

Megan acknowledged his skill as Katch began to blast away the invaders with as much regularity as she had, and a bit more dash. He likes to take chances, she mused as he narrowly missed being blown apart by laser fire in order to zap three ships in quick succession. As his score mounted, she stepped a bit closer to watch his technique.

At the brush of her arm against his, Megan noticed a quick, almost imperceptible break in his rhythm. Now, that was interesting, she reflected. Feeling an irrepressible surge of mischief, she edged slightly closer. There was another brief fluctuation in his timing. Softly, she touched her lips to his shoulder, then smiled up into his face. She heard rather than saw the explosion that marked his ship's untimely end.

Katch wasn't looking at the screen either, but at her. She saw something flash into his eyes—something hot, barely suppressed, before his hand released the control to dive into her hair.

"Cheat," he murmured.

For a moment, Megan forgot the cacophony of sound, forgot the crowds of people that milled around them. She was lost somewhere in those smoky gray eyes and her own giddy sense of power.

"Cheat?" she repeated, and her lips stayed slightly parted. "I don't know what you mean."

The hand on her hair tightened. He was struggling, she realized, surprised and excited. "I think you do," Katch said quietly. "And I think I'm going to have to be very careful now that you know just what you can do to me."

"Katch." Her gaze lowered to his mouth as the longings built. "Maybe I don't want you to be careful anymore."

Slowly, his hand slid out of her hair, over

her cheek, then dropped. "All the more reason I have to be," he muttered. "Come on." He took her arm and propelled her away from the machine. "Let's play something else."

Megan flowed with his mood, content just to be with him. They pumped tokens into machines and competed fiercely—as much with each other as with the computers. Megan felt the same lighthearted ease with him that she'd experienced that night at the carnival. Spending time with him was much like a trip on one of the wild, breathless rides at the park. Quick curves, fast hills, unexpected starts and stops. No one liked the windy power of a roller coaster better than Megan.

Hands on hips, she stood back as he consistently won coupons at Skee Ball. She watched another click off on the already lengthy strip as he tossed the ball neatly into the center hole.

"Don't you ever lose?" she demanded.

Katch tossed the next ball for another forty points. "I try not to make a habit of it. Wanna toss the last two?"

"No." She brushed imaginary lint from

her shirt. "You're having such a good time showing off."

With a laugh, Katch dumped the last two balls for ninety points, then leaned over to tear off his stream of coupons. "Just for that, I might not turn these in for your souvenir."

"These?" Megan gave the ream of thin cardboard an arched-brow look. "You were supposed to *buy* me a souvenir."

"I did." He grinned, rolling them up. "Indirectly." Slipping an arm companionably around her shoulder, he walked to the center counter where prizes were displayed. "Let's see...I've got two dozen. How about one of those six-function penknives?"

"Just who's this souvenir for?" Megan asked dryly as she scanned the shelves. "I like that little silk rose." She tapped the glass counter to indicate a small lapel pin. "I have all the tools I need," she added with an impish grin.

"Okay." Katch nodded to the woman behind the counter, then tore off all but four of the tickets. "That leaves us these. Ah..." With a quick scan of the shelves, he pointed. "That."

Thoughtfully, Megan studied the tiny

shell figure the woman lifted down. It seemed to be a cross between a duck and a penguin. "What're you going to do with that?"

"Give it to you." Katch handed over the rest of the tickets. "I'm a very generous man."

"I'm overwhelmed," she murmured. Megan turned it over in the palm of her hand as Katch pinned the rose to the collar of her shirt. "But what is it?"

"It's a mallard." Draping his arm over her shoulder again, he led her out of the arcade. "I'm surprised at your attitude. I figured, as an artist, you'd recognize its aesthetic value."

"*Hmm.*" Megan took another study, then slipped it into her pocket. "Well, I do recognize a certain winsome charm. And," she added, rising on her toes to kiss his cheek, "it was sweet of you to spend all your winnings on me."

Smiling, Katch ran a finger down her nose. "Is a kiss on the cheek the best you can do?"

"For a shell penguin it is."

"It's a mallard," he reminded her.

"Whatever." Laughing, Megan slipped an arm around his waist as they crossed the boardwalk and walked down the slope to the beach.

The moon was only a thin slice of white, but the stars were brilliant and mirrored in the water. There was a quiet swish of waves flowing and ebbing over the sand. Lovers walked here and there, arm in arm, talking quietly or not speaking at all. Children dashed along with flashlights bobbing, searching the sand and the surf for treasures.

Bending, Megan slipped out of her shoes and rolled up the hem of her jeans. In silent agreement, Katch followed suit. The water lapped cool over their ankles as they began to walk north, until the laughter and music from the boardwalk was only a background echo.

"Your sister's lovely," Megan said at length. "Just as you said."

"Jessica was always a beauty," he agreed absently. "A little hardheaded, but always a beauty."

"I saw your nieces at the park." Megan lifted her head so that the ocean breeze caught at her hair. "They had chocolate all over their faces."

"Typical." He laughed, running a hand up and down her arm as they walked. Megan felt the blood begin to hum beneath her flesh. "Before they left tonight, they were out digging for worms. I've been drafted to take them fishing tomorrow."

"You like children."

He twisted his head to glance down at her, but Megan was looking out to sea. "Yes. They're a constant adventure, aren't they?"

"I see so many of them in the park every summer, yet they never cease to amaze me." She turned back then with her slow, serious smile hovering on her lips. "And I see a fair number of harassed or long-suffering parents."

"When did you lose yours?"

He saw the flicker of surprise in her eyes before she looked down the stretch of beach again. "I was five."

"It's difficult for you to remember them."

"Yes. I have some vague memories—impressions really, I suppose. Pop has pictures, of course. When I see them, it always surprises me how young they were."

"It must have been hard on you," Katch murmured. "Growing up without them."

The gentleness in his voice had her turning back to him. They'd walked far down the beach so that the only light now came from the stars. His eyes caught the glitter of reflection as they held hers. "It would have been," Megan told him, "without Pop. He did much more than fill in." She stopped to take a step farther into the surf. The water frothed and bubbled over her skin. "One of my best memories is of him struggling to iron this pink organdy party dress. I was eight or nine, I think." With a shake of her head, she laughed and kicked the water. "I can still see him."

Katch's arms came around her waist, drawing her back against him. "So can I."

"He was standing there, struggling with frills and flounces—and swearing like a sailor because he didn't know I was there. I still love him for that," she murmured. "For just that."

Katch brushed his lips over the top of her hair. "And I imagine you told him not long afterward that you didn't care much for party dresses."

Surprised, Megan turned around. "How did you know that?"

"I know you." Slowly, he traced the shape of her face with his fingertip.

Frowning, she looked beyond his shoulder. "Am I so simple?"

"No." With his fingertip still on her jaw, he turned her face back to his. "You might say I've made a study of you."

She felt her blood begin to churn. "Why?"

Katch shook his head and combed his fingers through her hair. "No questions tonight," he said quietly. "I don't have the answers yet."

"No questions," she agreed, then rose on her toes to meet his mouth with hers.

It was a soft, exploring kiss—a kiss of renewal. Megan could taste the gentleness. For the moment, he seemed to prize her, to find her precious and rare. He held her lightly, as though she would break at the slightest pressure. Her lips parted, and it was she who entered his mouth first, teasing his tongue with hers. His sound of pleasure warmed her. The water swayed, soft and cool, on her calves.

She ran her hands up his back, letting her strong, artist's fingers trail under his hair to caress the nape of his neck. There was tension there, and she murmured against his lips as if to soothe it. Megan felt both his resistance and the tightening of his fingers against her skin. Her body pressed more demandingly into his.

Passion began to smolder quietly. Megan knew she was drawing it from him without his complete consent. The wonder of her own power struck her like a flash. He was holding back, letting her set the pace, but she could feel the near-violence of need in him. It tempted her. She wanted to undermine his control as he had undermined hers. She wanted to make him need as blindly as she needed. It wasn't possible to make him love her, but she could make him want. If it was all she could have from him, then she would be satisfied with his desire.

Megan felt his control slipping. His arms tightened around her, drawing her close so they were silhouetted as one. The kiss grew harder, more urgent. He lifted a hand to her hair, gripping it, pulling her head back as if now he would take command. There was fire now, burning brightly. Heat rose in her, smoking through her blood. She caught his bottom lip between her teeth and heard his quiet moan. Abruptly, he drew her away.

"Meg."

She waited, having no idea what she wanted him to say. Her head was tossed back, her face open to his, her hair free to the breeze. She felt incredibly strong. His eyes were nearly black, searching her face deeply. She could feel his breath feather, warm and uneven, on her lips.

"Meg." He repeated her name, bringing his hands back to her shoulders slowly. "I have to go now."

Daring more than she would have believed possible, Megan pressed her lips to his again. Hers were soft and hungry and drew instant response from him. "Is that what you want?" she murmured. "Do you want to leave me now?"

His fingers tightened on her arms convulsively, then he pulled her away again. "You know the answer to that," he said roughly. "What are you trying to do, make me crazy?"

"Maybe." Desire still churned in her. It

smoldered in her eyes as they met his. "Maybe I am."

He caught her against him, close and tight. She could feel the furious race of his heart against hers. His control, she knew, balanced on a razor's edge. Their lips were only a whisper apart.

"There'll be a time," he said softly, "I swear it, when it'll just be you and me. Next time, the very next time, Meg. Remember it."

It took no effort to keep her eyes level with his. The power was still flowing through her. "Is that a warning?"

"Yes," he told her. "That's just what it is."

Chapter 11

It took two more days for Megan to finish the bust of Katch. She tried, when it was time, to divorce herself from emotion and judge it objectively.

She'd been right to choose wood. It was warmer than stone. With her tongue caught between her teeth, she searched for flaws in her workmanship. Megan knew without conceit it was one of her better pieces. Perhaps the best.

The face wasn't stylishly handsome, but strong and compelling. Humor was expressed in the tilt of the brows and mouth.

She ran her fingertips over his lips. An incredibly expressive mouth, she mused, remembering the taste and texture. I know just how it looks when he's amused or angry or aroused. And his eyes. Hers drifted up to linger. I know how they look, how they change shades and expression with a mood. Light for pleasure, turning smoky in anger, darker in passion.

I know his face as well as my own...but I still don't know his mind. That's still a stranger. With a sigh she folded her arms on the table and lowered her chin to them.

Would he ever permit me to know him? she wondered. Tenderly, she touched a lock of the disordered hair. Jessica knows him, probably better than anyone else. If he loved someone...

What would happen if I drew up the courage to tell him that I love him? What would happen if I simply walked up to him and said *I love you?* Demanding nothing, expecting nothing. Doesn't he perhaps have the right to know? Isn't love too special, too rare to be closed up? Then Megan imagined his eyes with pity in them.

"I couldn't bear it," she murmured, lowering her forehead to Katch's wooden one. "I just couldn't bear it." A knock interrupted her soul-searching. Quickly, Megan composed her features and swiveled in her chair. "Come in."

Her grandfather entered, his fishing cap perched jauntily on his mane of white hair. "How do you feel about fresh fish for supper?" His grin told her that his early morning expedition had been a success. Megan cocked her head.

"I could probably choke down a few bites." She smiled, pleased to see his eyes sparkling and color in his cheeks. She sprang up and wound her arms around his neck as she had done as a child. "Oh, I love you, Pop!"

"Well, well." He patted her hair, both surprised and pleased. "I love you too, Megan. I guess I should bring you home trout more often."

She lifted her face from the warm curve of his neck and smiled at him. "It doesn't take much to make me happy."

His eyes sobered as he tucked her hair behind her ear. "No.... It never has." His wide, blunt hand touched her cheek.

"You've given me so much pleasure over the years, Megan, so much joy. I'm going to miss you when you're in New York."

"Oh, Pop." She buried her face again and clung. "It'll only be for a month or two, then I'll be home." She could smell the cherry-flavored scent of the tobacco he carried in his breast pocket. "You could even come with me—the season'll be over."

"Meg." He stopped her rambling and drew her up so that their eyes met. "This is a start for you. Don't put restrictions on it."

Shaking her head, Megan rose to pace nervously. "I'm not. I don't know what you mean..."

"You're going to make something of yourself, something important. You have talent." Pop glanced around the room at her work until his eyes rested on the bust of Katch. "You've got a life to start. I want you to go after it at full speed."

"You make it sound as if I'm not coming home." Megan turned and, seeing where his eyes rested, clasped her hands together. "I've just finished that." She moistened her lips and struggled to keep her voice casual. "It's rather good, don't you think?"

"Yes, I think it's very good." He looked at her then. "Sit down, Megan, I need to talk to you."

She recognized the tone and tensed. Without a word, she obeyed, going to the chair across from him. Pop waited until she was settled, then studied her face carefully.

"Awhile back," he began, "I told you things change. Most of your life, it's been just the two of us. We needed each other, depended on each other. We had the park to keep a roof over our heads and to give us something to work for." His tone softened. "There hasn't been one minute in the eighteen years I've had you with me that you've been a burden. You've kept me young. I've watched you through all the stages of growing up, and each time, you've made me more proud of you. It's time for the next change."

Because her throat was dry as dust, Megan swallowed. "I don't understand what you're trying to tell me."

"It's time you moved out into the world, Megan, time I let you." Pop reached in the pocket of his shirt and took out carefully folded papers. After spreading them out, he handed them to Megan.

She hesitated before accepting them, her eyes clinging to his. The instant she saw the papers, she knew what they were. But when she read, she read each sentence, each word, until the finish. ‘‘So,’’ she said, dry-eyed, dry-voiced. ‘‘You’ve sold it to him.’’

‘‘When I sign the papers,’’ Pop told her, ‘‘and you witness it.’’ He saw the look of devastation in her eyes. ‘‘Megan, hear me out. I’ve given this a lot of thought.’’ Pop took the papers and set them on the table, then gripped her hands. ‘‘Katch isn’t the first to approach me about selling, and this isn’t the first time I’ve considered it. Everything didn’t fit the way I wanted before—this time it does.’’

‘‘What fits?’’ she demanded, feeling her eyes fill.

‘‘It’s the right man, Meg, the right time.’’ He soothed her hands, hating to watch her distress. ‘‘I knew it when all those repairs fell on me. I’m ready to let it go, to let someone younger take over so I can go fishing. That’s what I want now, Megan, a boat and a rod. And he’s the man I want taking over.’’ He paused, fumbling in his pocket for a handkerchief to wipe his eyes. ‘‘I told you I trusted him and that still holds. Managing the park for Katch won't keep me from my fishing, and I'll have the stimulation without the headaches. And you," he continued, brushing tears from her cheeks, "you need to cut the strings. You can't do what you're meant to do if you're struggling to balance books and make payroll."

"If it's what you want," Megan began, but Pop cut her off.

"No, it has to be what you want. That's why the last lines are still blank." He looked at her with his deep-set eyes sober and quiet. "I won't sign it, Megan, unless you agree. It has to be what's best for both of us."

Megan stood again, and he released her hands to let her walk to the window. At the moment, she was unable to understand her own feelings. She knew agreeing to do a show in New York was a giant step away from the life she had led. And the park was a major part of that life. She knew in order to pursue her own career, she couldn't continue to tie herself to the business end of Joyland.

The park had been security—her responsibility, her second home—as the man behind her had been both mother and father to her. She remembered the look of weariness on his face when he had come to tell her that the park needed money. Megan knew the hours and endless demands that summer would bring.

He was entitled to live his winter years as he chose, she decided. With less worry, less responsibility. He was entitled to fish, and to sleep late and putter around his azaleas. What right did she have to deny him that because she was afraid to cut the last tie with her childhood? He was right, it was time for the change.

Slowly, she walked to her workbox and searched out a pen. Going to Pop, Megan held it out to him. ''Sign it. We'll have champagne with the trout.''

Pop took the pen, but kept his eyes on her. ''Are you sure, Meg?''

She nodded, as sure for him as she was uncertain for herself. ''Positive.'' She smiled and watched the answering light in his eyes before he bent over the paper.

He signed his name with a flourish, then passed her the pen so that she could witness his signature. Megan wrote her name in clear, distinct letters, not allowing her hand to tremble.

"I suppose I should call Katch," Pop mused, sighing as though a weight had been lifted. "Or take the papers to him."

"I'll take them." Carefully, Megan folded them again. "I'd like to talk to him."

"That's a good idea. Take the pickup," he suggested as she headed for the door. "It looks like rain."

Megan was calm by the time she reached Katch's house. The papers were tucked securely in the back pocket of her cutoffs. She pulled the truck behind his car and climbed out.

The air was deadly still and heavy, nearly shimmering with restrained rain. The clouds overhead were black and bulging with it. She walked to the front door and knocked as she had many days before. As before, there was no answer. She walked back down the steps and skirted the house.

There was no sign of him in the yard, no sound but the voice of the sea muffled by the tall hedges. He'd planted a willow, a young, slender one near the slope which led to the beach. The earth was still dark around it, freshly turned. Unable to resist, Megan walked to it, wanting to touch the tender young leaves. It was no taller than she, but she knew one day it would be magnificent...sweeping, graceful, a haven of shade in the summer. Instinct made her continue down the slope to the beach.

Hands in his pockets, he stood, watching the swiftly incoming tide. As if sensing her, he turned.

"I was standing here thinking of you," he said. "Did I wish you here?"

She took the papers and held them out to him. "It's yours," she told him calmly. "Just as you wanted."

He didn't even glance down at the papers, but she saw the shift of expression in his eyes. "I'd like to talk to you, Meg. Let's go inside."

"No." She stepped back to emphasize her refusal. "There really isn't anything more to say."

"That might be true for you, but I have a great deal to say. And you're going to listen." Impatience intruded into his tone. Megan heard it as she felt the sudden gust of wind which broke the calm.

"I don't want to listen to you, Katch. This is what Pop wants, too." She thrust the papers into his hands as the first spear of lightning split the sky. "Take them, will you?"

"Megan, wait." He grabbed her arm as she turned to go. The thunder all but drowned out his words.

"I will not wait!" she tossed back, jerking her arm free. "And stop grabbing me. You have what you wanted—you don't need me anymore."

Katch swore, thrust the papers in his pocket and caught her again before she'd taken three steps. He whirled her back around. "You're not that big an idiot."

"Don't tell me how big an idiot I am." She tried to shake herself loose.

"We have to talk. I have things to say to you. It's important." A gust of wind whipped violently across Megan's face.

"Don't you understand a simple no?" she shouted at him, her voice competing with pounding surf and rising wind. She struggled against his hold. "I don't want to talk. I don't want to hear what you have to say. I don't *care* about what you have to say."

The rain burst from the clouds and poured over them. Instantly, they were drenched.

"Tough," he retorted, every bit as angry as she. "Because you're going to hear it. Now, let's go inside."

He started to pull her across the sand, but she swung violently away and freed herself. Rain gushed down in torrents, sheeting around them. "No!" she shouted. "I won't go inside with you."

"Oh yes you will," he corrected.

"What are you going to do?" she demanded. "Drag me by the hair?"

"Don't tempt me." Katch took her hand again only to have her pull away. "All right," he said. "Enough." In a swift move that caught her off guard, he swept her up into his arms.

"Put me down." Megan wriggled and kicked, blind with fury. He ignored her, dealing with her struggles by shifting her closer and climbing the slope without any apparent effort. Lightning and thunder warred around them. "Oh, I hate you!" she claimed as he walked briskly across the lawn.

"Good. That's a start." Katch pushed

open the door with his hip, then continued through the kitchen and into the living room. A trail of rain streamed behind them. Without ceremony, he dumped her on the sofa. "Sit still," he ordered before she could regain her breath, "and just be quiet a minute." He walked to the hearth. Taking a long match, he set fire to the paper waiting beneath kindling and logs. Dry wood crackled and caught almost instantly.

Regaining her breath, Megan rose and bounded for the door. Katch stopped her before her fingers touched the knob. He held her by the shoulders with her back to the door. "I warn you, Meg, my tolerance is at a very low ebb. Don't push me."

"You don't frighten me," she told him, impatiently flipping her dripping hair from her eyes.

"I'm not trying to frighten you. I'm trying to reason with you. But you're too stubborn to shut up and listen."

Her eyes widened with fresh fury. "Don't you talk to me that way! I don't have to take that."

"Yes, you do." Deftly, he reached in her

right front pocket and pulled out the truck keys. "As long as I have these."

"I can walk," she tossed back as he pocketed them himself.

"In this rain?"

Megan hugged her arms as she began to shiver. "Let me have my keys."

Instead of answering, he pulled her across the room in front of the fire. "You're freezing. You'll have to get out of those wet clothes."

"I will not. You're crazy if you think I'm going to take off my clothes in your house."

"Suit yourself." He stripped off his own sopping T-shirt and tossed it angrily aside. "You're the most hardheaded, single-minded, stubborn woman I know."

"Thanks." Barely, Megan controlled the urge to sneeze. "Is that all you wanted to say?"

"No." He walked to the fire again. "That's just the beginning—there's a lot more. Sit down."

"Then maybe I'll have my say first." Chills were running over her skin, and she struggled not to tremble. "I was wrong about you in a lot of ways. You're not lazy or careless or glory-seeking. And you were certainly honest with me.'' She wiped water from her eyes, a mixture of rain and tears. ''You told me up front that you intended to have the park, and it seems perhaps for the best. What happened between then and now is my fault for being foolish enough to let you get to me.'' Megan swallowed, wanting to salvage a little pride. ''But then you're a difficult man to ignore. Now you have what you wanted, and it's over and done.''

''I only have part of what I wanted.'' Katch came to her and gathered her streaming hair in his hand. ''Only part, Meg.''

She looked at him, too tired to argue. ''Can't you just let me be?'' she asked.

''Let you be? Do you know how many times I've walked that beach at three in the morning because wanting you kept me awake and aching? Do you know how hard it was for me to let you go every time I had you in my arms?'' The fingers in her hair tightened, pulled her closer.

Her eyes were huge now while chills shivered over her skin. *What was he saying?* She couldn't risk asking, couldn't risk wondering. Abruptly, he cursed her and dragged her into his arms.

Thin wet clothes were no barrier to his hands. He molded her breasts even while his mouth ravished hers. She made no protest when he lowered her to the floor, as his fingers worked desperately at the buttons of her blouse. Her chilled wet skin turned to fire under his fingertips. His mouth was hungry, hot as it roamed to her throat and downward.

There was only the crackle of wood and the splash of rain on the windows to mix with their breathing. A log shifted in the grate.

Megan heard him take a long, deep breath. ''I'm sorry. I wanted to talk—there are things I need to tell you. But I need you. I've kept it pent up a long time.''

Need. Her mind centered on the word. Need was infinitely different from want. Need was more personal—still apart from love—but she let her heart grip the word.

''It's all right.'' Megan started to sit up, but he leaned over her. Sparks flicked inside her at the touch of naked flesh to naked flesh. ''Katch…''

''Please, Meg. Listen to me.''

She searched his face, noting the uncharacteristically grave eyes and mouth. Whatever he had to say was important to him. "All right," she said, quieter now, ready. "I'll listen."

"When I first saw you, the first minute, I wanted you. You know that." His voice was low, but without its usual calm. Something boiled just under the surface. "The first night we were together, you intrigued me as much as you attracted me. I thought it would be a simple matter to have you…a casual, pleasant affair for a few weeks."

"I know," she spoke softly, trying not to be wounded by the truth.

"No—shh." He lay a finger over her lips a moment. "You don't know. It stopped being simple almost immediately. When I had you here for dinner, and you asked to stay…" He paused, brushing wet strands of hair from her cheeks. "I couldn't let you, and I wasn't completely sure why. I wanted you—wanted you more than any woman I'd ever touched, any woman I'd ever dreamed about—but I couldn't take you."

"Katch…" Megan shook her head, not

certain she was strong enough to hear the words.

"Please." She had closed her eyes, and Katch waited until she opened them again before he continued. "I tried to stay away from you, Meg. I tried to convince myself I was imagining what was happening to me. Then you were charging across the lawn, looking outraged and so beautiful I couldn't think of anything. Just looking at you took my breath away." While she lay motionless, he lifted her hand and pressed it to his lips. The gesture moved her unbearably.

"Don't," she murmured. "Please."

Katch stared into her eyes for a long moment, then released her hand. "I wanted you," he went on in a voice more calm than his eyes. "Needed you, was furious with you because of it." He rested his forehead on hers and shut his eyes. "I never wanted to hurt you, Meg—to frighten you."

Megan lay still, aware of the turmoil in him. Firelight played over the skin on his arms and back.

"It seemed impossible that I could be so involved I couldn't pull away," he continued. "But you were so tangled up in my thoughts, so wound up in my dreams. There wasn't any escape. The other night, after I'd taken you home, I finally admitted to myself I didn't want an escape. Not this time. Not from you.'' He lifted his head and looked down at her again. ''I have something for you, but first I want you to know I'd decided against buying the park until your grandfather came to me last night. I didn't want that between us, but it was what he wanted. What he thought was best for you and for himself. But if it hurts you, I'll tear the papers up.''

''No.'' Megan gave a weary sigh. ''I know it's best. It's just like losing someone you love. Even when you know it's the best thing, it still hurts.'' The outburst seemed to have driven out the fears and the pain. ''Please, I don't want you to apologize. I was wrong, coming here this way, shouting at you. Pop has every right to sell the park, and you have every right to buy it.'' She sighed, wanting explanations over. ''I suppose I felt betrayed somehow and didn't want to think it all through.''

''And now?''

''And now I'm ashamed of myself for acting like a fool.'' She managed a weak smile.

"I'd like to get up and go home. Pop'll be worried."

"Not just yet." When Katch leaned back on his heels to take something from his pocket, Megan sat up, pushing her wet, tangled hair behind her. He held a box, small and thin. Briefly, he hesitated before offering it to her. Puzzled, both by the gift and by the tension she felt emanating from him, Megan opened it. Her breath caught.

It was a dark, smoky green emerald, square cut and exquisite in its simplicity. Stunned, Megan stared at it, then at Katch. She shook her head wordlessly.

"Katch." Megan shook her head again. "I don't understand…I can't accept this."

"Don't say no, Meg." Katch closed his hand over hers. "I don't handle rejection well." The words were light, but she recognized, and was puzzled by, the strain in the tone. A thought trembled in her brain, and her heart leaped with it.

She tried to be calm and keep her eyes steady on his. "I don't know what you're asking me."

His fingers tightened on hers. "Marry me. I love you."

Emotions ran riot through her. He must be joking, she thought quickly, though no hint of amusement showed in his eyes. His face was so serious, she reflected, and the words so simple. Where were the carelessly witty phrases, the glib charm? Shaken, Megan rose with the box held tightly in her hand. She needed to think.

Marriage. Never had she expected him to ask her to share a lifetime. What would life be like with him? *Like the roller coaster.* She knew it instantly. It would be a fast, furious ride, full of unexpected curves and indescribable thrills. And quiet moments too, she reflected. Precious, solitary moments which would make each new twist and turn more exciting.

Perhaps he had asked her this way, so simply, without any of the frills he could so easily provide because he was as vulnerable as she. What a thought that was! She lifted her fingers to her temple. David Katcherton vulnerable. And yet…Megan remembered what she had seen in his eyes.

I love you. The three simple words, words spoken every day by people everywhere, had changed her life forever. Megan turned, then walking back, knelt beside him. Her eyes were as grave, as searching as his. She held the box out, then spoke quickly as she saw the flicker of desperation.

"It belongs on the third finger of my left hand."

Then she was caught against him, her mouth silenced bruisingly. "Oh, Meg," he murmured her name as he rained kisses on her face. "I thought you were turning me down."

"How could I?" She wound her arms around his neck and tried to stop his roaming mouth with her own. "I love you, Katch." The words were against his lips. "Desperately, completely. I'd prepared myself for a slow death when you were ready to walk away."

"No one's going to walk away now." They lay on the floor again, and he buried his face in her rain-scented hair. "We'll go to New Orleans. A quick honeymoon before you have to come back and work on the show. In the spring, we'll go to Paris." He lifted his face and looked down on her. "I've thought about you and me in Paris, making love. I want to see your face in the morning when the light's soft."

She touched his cheek. "Soon," she whispered. "Marry me soon. I want to be with you."

He picked up the box that had fallen beside them. Drawing out the ring, he slipped it on her finger. Then, gripping her hand with his, he looked down at her.

"Consider it binding, Meg," he told her huskily. "You can't get away now."

"I'm not going anywhere." She lifted her mouth to meet his kiss.

Epilogue

Nervously, Megan twisted the emerald on her finger and tried to drink the champagne Jessica had pushed into her hand. She felt as though the smile had frozen onto her face. People, she thought. She'd never expected so many people. What was she doing, standing in a Manhattan gallery pretending she was an artist? What she wanted to do was creep into the back room and be very, very sick.

"Here now, Meg." Pop strolled over beside her, looking oddly distinguished in his best—and only—black suit. "You should try one of these—tasty little things." He held out a canapé.

"No." Megan felt her stomach roll and shook her head. "No, thanks. I'm so glad you flew up for the weekend."

"Think I'd miss my granddaughter's big night?" He ate the canapé and grinned. "How about this turnout?"

"I feel like an impostor," Megan murmured, smiling gamely as a man in a flowing cape moved past her to study one of her marble pieces.

"Never seen you look prettier." Pop plucked at the sleeve of her dress, a swirl of watercolored silk. "'Cept maybe at your wedding."

"I wasn't nearly as scared then." She made a quick scan of the crowd and found only strangers. "Where's Katch?"

"Last time I saw him he was cornered by a couple of ritzy-looking people. Didn't I hear Jessica say you were supposed to mingle?"

"Yes." Megan made a small, frustrated sound. "I don't think I can move."

"Now, Meg, I've never known you to be chicken-hearted."

With her mouth half-opened in protest, she watched him walk away. *Chicken-hearted,* she repeated silently. Straightening her shoulders, she drank some champagne. All right then, she decided, she wouldn't stand there cowering in the corner. If she was going to be shot down, she'd face it head on. Moving slowly, and with determined confidence, Megan walked toward the buffet.

"You're the artist, aren't you?"

Megan turned to face a striking old woman in diamonds and black silk. "Yes," she said with a fractional lift of her chin. "I am."

"Hmmm." The woman took Megan in with a long, sweeping glance. "I noticed the study of the girl with the sand castle isn't for sale."

"No, it's my husband's." After two months, the words still brought the familiar warmth to her blood. *Katch, my husband.* Megan's eyes darted around the room to find him.

"A pity," the woman in black commented.

"I beg your pardon?"

"I said it's a pity—I wanted it."

"You—" Stunned, Megan stared at her. "You wanted it?"

"I've purchased 'The Lovers,'" she went on as Megan only gaped. "An excellent piece, but I want to commission you to do another sand castle. I'll contact you through Jessica."

"Yes, of course." *Commission?* Megan thought numbly as she automatically offered her hand. "Thank you," she added as the woman swept away.

"Miriam Tailor Marcus," a voice whispered beside her ear. "A tough nut to crack."

Megan half turned and grabbed Katch's arm. "Katch, that woman, she—"

"Miriam Tailor Marcus," he repeated and bent down to kiss her astonished mouth. "And I heard. I've just been modestly accepting compliments on my contribution to the art world." He touched the rim of his glass to hers. "Congratulations, love."

"They like my work?" she whispered.

"If you hadn't been so busy trying to be invisible, you'd know you're a smashing success. Walk around with me," he told her as he took her hand. "And look at all the little blue dots under your sculptures that mean SOLD."

"They're buying?" Megan gave a wondering laugh as she spotted sale after sale. "They're really buying them?"

"Jessica's frantically trying to keep up. Three people've tried to buy the alabaster piece she bought from you herself—at twice what you charged her. And if you don't talk to a couple of the art critics soon, she's going to go crazy."

"I can't believe it."

"Believe it." He brought Megan's hand to his lips. "I'm very proud of you, Meg."

Tears welled up, threatening to brim over. "I have to get out of here for a minute," she whispered. "Please."

Without a word, Katch maneuvered his way through the crowd, taking Megan into the storage room and shutting the door behind them.

"This is silly," she said immediately as the tears rolled freely down her cheeks. "I'm an idiot. I have everything I've ever dreamed of and I'm crying in the back room. I'd have handled failure better than this."

"Megan." With a soft laugh, he gathered her close. "I love you."

"It doesn't seem real," she said with a quaver in her voice. "Not just the showing…it's everything. I see your ring on my finger and I keep wondering when I'm going to wake up. I can't believe that—"

His mouth silenced her. With a low, melting sigh, she dissolved against him. Even after all the days of her marriage, and all the intimate nights, he could still turn her to putty with only his mouth. The tears vanished as her blood began to swim. Pulling him closer, she let her hands run up the sides of his face and into his hair.

"It's real," he murmured against her mouth. "Believe it." Tilting his head, he changed the angle of the kiss and took her deeper. "It's real every night when you're in my arms, and every morning when you wake there." Katch drew her away slowly, then kissed both her damp cheeks until her lashes fluttered up. "Tonight," he said with a smile, "I'm going to make love to the newest star in the New York art world. And when she's still riding high over the reviews in the morning papers, I'm going to make love to her all over again."

"How soon can we slip away?"

Laughing, he caught her close for a hard kiss. "Don't tempt me. Jessica'd skin us both if we didn't stay until the gallery closes tonight. Now, fix your face and go bask in the admiration for a while. It's good for the soul."

"Katch." Megan stopped him before he could open the door. "There's one piece I didn't put out tonight."

Curious, he lifted a brow. "Oh?"

"Yes, well..." A faint color rose to her cheeks. "I was afraid things might not go well, and I thought I could handle the criticism. But this piece—I knew I couldn't bear to have anyone say it was a poor attempt or amateurish."

Puzzled, he slipped his hands into his pockets. "Have I seen it?"

"No." She shook her head, tossing her bangs out of her eyes. "I'd wanted to give it to you as a wedding present, but everything happened so fast and it wasn't finished. After all," she added with a grin, "we were only engaged for three days."

“Two days longer than if you’d agreed to fly to Vegas,” he pointed out. “All in all, I was very patient.”

“Be that as it may, I didn’t have time until later to finish it. Then I was so nervous about the showing that I couldn’t give it to you.” She took a deep breath. “I’d like you to have it now, tonight, while I’m feeling—really feeling like an artist.”

“Is it here?”

Turning around, Megan reached up on the shelf where the bust was carefully covered in cloth. Wordlessly, she handed it to him. Katch removed the cloth, then stared down into his own face.

Megan had polished the wood very lightly, wanting it to carry that not-quite-civilized aura she perceived in the model. It had his cockiness, his confidence and the warmth the artist had sensed in him before the woman had. He stared at it for so long, she felt the nerves begin to play in her stomach again. Then he looked up, eyes dark, intense.

“Meg.”

“I don’t want to put it out on display,”

she said hurriedly. "It's too personal to me. There were times," she began as she took the bust from him and ran a thumb down a cheekbone, "when I was working on the clay model, that I wanted to smash it." With a half-laugh, she set it down on a small table. "I couldn't. When I started it, I told myself the only reason I kept thinking about you was because you had the sort of face I'd like to sculpt." She lifted her eyes then to find his fixed on hers. "I fell in love with you sitting in my studio, while my hands were forming your face." Stepping forward, Megan lifted her hands and traced her fingers over the planes and bones under his flesh. "I thought I couldn't love you more than I did then. I was wrong."

"Meg." Katch brought his hands to hers, pressing her palms to his lips. "You leave me speechless."

"Just love me."

"Always."

"That just might be long enough." Megan sighed as she rested her head against his shoulder. "And I think I'll be able to handle success knowing it."

Katch slipped an arm around her waist as he opened the door. "Let's go have some more champagne. It's a night for celebrations."

* * * * *

NORA ROBERTS

THE BEST MISTAKE

Harlequin Mills & Boon

First Published 1994
Second Australian Paperback Edition 2004
ISBN 0 733 55157 2

Published by
Harlequin Mills & Boon
3 Gibbes Street
CHATSWOOD NSW 2067
AUSTRALIA

Printed and bound in Australia by
McPherson's Printing Group

Chapter 1

No one answered the door. Coop glanced at the scrawled note in his hand to make sure he had the right address. It checked out, and since the tidy two-story Tudor in the neat, tree-lined neighborhood was precisely what he was after, he knocked again. Loudly.

There was a car in the drive, an aging station wagon that could use a good wash and a little bodywork. Somebody was in there, he thought, scowling up at the second-floor window, where music pumped out—high-volume rock with a thumping backbeat. He stuffed the note and his hands in his pockets and took a moment to survey the surroundings.

The house was trim, set nicely off the road behind clipped bayberry hedges. The flower garden, in which spring blossoms were beginning to thrive, was both colorful and just wild enough not to look static.

Not that he was a big flower lover, but there *was* something to be said for ambience.

There was a shiny red tricycle beside the driveway, and that made him a little uneasy. He wasn't particularly fond of kids. Not that he disliked them. It was just that they always seemed a kind of foreign entity to him, like aliens from an outlying planet: they spoke a different language, had a different culture. And, well, they were short, and usually sticky.

Still, the ad had talked of quiet, privacy, and a convenient distance from Baltimore. That was exactly what he was looking for.

He knocked again, only to have a thundering wave of music wash out the window over him. The rock didn't bother him. At least he understood it. But he wasn't a man to kick his heels outside a closed door for long, so he tried the knob.

When it turned, he pushed the door open and walked in. In an old habit, he pushed back the dark hair that fell over his forehead and scanned the none-too-neat living room he'd entered.

There was a lot of clutter, and he, a bachelor who'd spent a great deal of his thirty-two years living alone, wondered over it. He wasn't fussy or obsessive, he often told himself. It was simply that everything had a place, and it was easier to find if it had been put there. Obviously his prospective landlord didn't agree.

There were toys that went along with the tricycle outside, piles of magazines and newspapers, a pint-size fielder's cap that declared for the O's.

At least the kid had taste, Coop decided, and moved on.

There was a small powder room done in an amazing combination of purple and green, and a den that had been converted into a makeshift office. File drawers were open, papers spilling out. In the kitchen dishes waited in the sink to be washed, and lurid drawings, created by a child with a wild imagination, decorated the front of the refrigerator.

Maybe, he thought, it was just as well no one had answered the door.

He considered backtracking and wandering upstairs. As long as he was here, it made sense to check the rest of the place out. Instead, he stepped outside to get the lay of the land. He spotted open wooden steps leading to a short deck. The private entrance the ad had mentioned, he mused, and climbed.

The glass door was open, and the music rolling through it was overwhelming. He caught the smell of fresh paint, one he'd always enjoyed, and stepped inside.

The open area combined kitchen and living space cleverly enough. The appliances weren't new, but they were gleaming. The tile floor had been scrubbed recently enough for him to identify pine cleaner beneath the scent of paint.

Feeling more hopeful, he followed the music, snooping a bit as he went. The bathroom was as scrupulously clean as the kitchen, and, fortunately, a plain glossy white. Beside the sink was a book on home repair, open to the plumbing section. Wary, Coop turned on the tap. When the water flowed out fast and clear, he nodded, satisfied.

A small room with definite office potential and a nice view of the yard was across the hall. The ad had claimed two bedrooms.

The music led him to it, a fair-sized room that fronted the house, with space enough for his California king. The floor, which seemed to be a random-width oak in good condition, was covered with splattered drop cloths. There were paint cans, trays, brushes, extra rollers. A laborer in baggy overalls and bare feet completed the picture. Despite the hair-concealing cap and oversize denim, Coop recognized a woman when he saw one.

She was tall, and the bare feet on the stepladder were long and narrow and decorated with paint splotches and hot-pink toenails. She sang, badly, along with the music.

Coop rapped on the door jamb. ''Excuse me.''

She went on painting, her hips moving rhythmically as she started on the ceiling border. Stepping across the drop cloths, Coop tapped her on the back.

She screamed, jumped and turned all at once.

Though he was quick on his feet, he wasn't fast enough to avoid the slap of the paintbrush across his cheek.

He swore and jerked backward, then forward again to catch her before she tumbled off the ladder. He had a quick, and not unpleasant, impression of a slim body, a pale, triangular face dominated by huge, long-lashed brown eyes, and the scent of honeysuckle.

Then he was grunting and stumbling backward, clutching the stomach her elbow had jammed into. She yelled something while he fought to get his breath back.

"Are you crazy?" he managed, then shot up a hand as she hefted a can, slopping paint over the sides as she prepared to use it as a weapon. "Lady, if you throw that at me, I'm going to have to hurt you."

"What?" she shouted.

"I said, don't throw that. I'm here about the ad."

"What?" she shouted again. Her eyes were still wide and full of panic, and she looked capable of anything.

"The ad, damn it." Still rubbing his stomach, Coop marched to the portable stereo and shut it off. "I'm here about the ad," he repeated, his voice loud in the sudden silence.

The big brown eyes narrowed with suspicion. "What ad?"

"The apartment." He swiped a hand over his cheek,

studied the smear of white on it, and swore again. "The apartment."

"Really?" She kept her eyes glued to his. He looked tough, she thought. Like a brawler with those broad shoulders, lean athletic build and long legs. His eyes, a light, almost translucent green, looked anything but friendly, and the faded Baltimore Orioles T-shirt and battered jeans didn't contribute any sense of respectability. She figured she could outrun him, and she could certainly outscream him. "The ad doesn't start to run until tomorrow."

"Tomorrow?" Nonplussed, he reached into his pocket for his scribbled note. "This is the right address. The ad was for this place."

She stood her ground. "It doesn't run until tomorrow, so I don't see how you could know about it."

"I work at the paper." Moving cautiously, he held out the note. "Since I've been looking for a place, I asked one of the girls in Classifieds to keep an eye out." He glanced down at his note again. "Two-bedroom apartment on second floor, private entrance, quiet neighborhood convenient for commuters."

She only continued to frown at him. "That's right."

Realizing his inside track wasn't strictly ethical, he winced. "Look, I guess she got a little overenthusiastic. I gave her a couple of tickets to a game, and she must've figured she'd do me a favor and pass the information along a little early."

When he saw that her grip on the can had relaxed, he tried a smile. "I knocked, then I came around back." Probably best not to mention he'd wandered through the house first.

"The ad didn't run the address."

"I work at the paper," he repeated. He was taking a good look at her now. There was something vaguely familiar about her face. And what a face it was. All slashing cheekbones and liquid eyes, that creamy porcelain skin women's face cream ads always raved about. Her mouth was wide, with an alluringly full lower lip. At the moment, the face continued to frown.

"They had the address for billing," he continued. "Since I had a couple of hours, I thought I'd come by and check it out. Look, I can come back tomorrow, if you'd feel more comfortable. But I'm here now." He shrugged. "I can show you my press pass."

He pulled it out for her, and was pleased when she narrowed her eyes to study it. "I do a column. J. Cooper McKinnon on sports. 'All in the Game'?"

"Oh." It meant nothing to her. The sports page wasn't her choice of reading material. But the smile had appeased her. He didn't look so much like a thug when he smiled. And the smear of paint decorating the lean, tanned face added just enough comedy to soothe her. "I guess it's all right, then. I wasn't expecting to show the apartment for a couple of days yet. It's not ready." She held up the can, set it down again. "I'm still painting."

"I noticed."

She laughed at that. It was a full-throated, smoky sound that went with the natural huskiness of her voice. "Guess you did. I'm Zoe Fleming." She crouched down to dampen a rag with paint remover.

"Thanks." He rubbed the rag over his cheek. "The ad said immediate occupancy."

"Well, I figured I'd be finished in here by tomorrow, when the ad was scheduled to run. Are you from the area?"

"I've got a place downtown. I'm looking for something with a little more space, a little more atmosphere."

"This is a pretty good-sized apartment. It was converted about eight years ago. The guy who owned it had it done for his son, and when he died, the son sold it and moved to California. He wanted to write sitcoms."

Coop walked over to check out the view. He moved fluidly, Zoe thought, like a man who knew how to stay light and ready on his feet. She'd had the impression of wiry strength when her body tumbled into his. And good strong hands. Quick ones, too. She pursed her lips. It might be handy to have a man around.

"Is it just you, Mr. McKinnon?" She thought wistfully how nice it would be if he had a family—another child for Keenan to play with.

"Just me." The place felt right, he decided. It

would be good to get out of a box that was just one more box in a building of boxes, to smell grass now and then. Barbecue smoke. "I can move in over the weekend."

She hadn't thought it would be so easy, and she nibbled her lip as she thought it through. She'd never been a landlady before, but she'd been a tenant, and she figured she knew the ropes. "I'll need first and last months' rent."

"Yeah."

"And, ah, references."

"I'll give you the number of the management company that handles my building. You can call Personnel at the paper. Have you got a lease for me to sign?"

She didn't. She'd checked out a book from the library, and she'd meant to type up a scaled-down copy of a lease from it the next morning. "I'll have it tomorrow. Don't you want to look at the rest of the apartment, ask any questions?" She'd been practicing her landlady routine for days.

"I've seen it. It's fine."

"Well." That deflated her a bit. "I guess I can cancel the ad."

There was a sound like a herd of rampaging elephants. Zoe glanced toward the open door and crouched to intercept the missile that hurtled through.

It was a boy, Coop saw when she scooped the child up. He had glossy golden hair, red sneakers, and jeans that were streaked with some unidentifiable substance that looked like it would easily transfer to other surfaces. He carried a plastic lunch box with a picture of some apocalyptic space battle on it, and a sheet of drawing paper that was grimy at the edges.

"I drew the ocean," he announced. "And a million people got ate by sharks."

"Gruesome." Zoe shuddered obligingly before accepting his sloppy kiss. She set him down to admire the drawing. "These are really big sharks," she said, cagily distinguishing the shark blobs from the people blobs.

"They're monster sharks. Mutant monster sharks. They have teeth."

"So I see. Keenan, this is Mr. McKinnon. Our new tenant."

Keenan wrapped one arm around Zoe's leg for security as he eyed the stranger. His eyes were working their way up to Coop's face when they lit on the T-shirt. "That's baseball. I'm gonna learn. Mama's getting a book so's she can teach me."

A book. Coop barely checked a snort. As if you could learn the greatest game invented by a man from a book. What kind of nerd did the kid have for a father?

"Great." It was all Coop intended to say. He'd always thought it wise to avoid entangling himself in a conversation with anyone under sixteen.

Keenan had other ideas. "If you're going to live here, you have to pay rent. Then we can pay the mortgage and stuff and go to Disney World."

What *was* the kid? An accountant?

"Okay, old man." Zoe laughed and ruffled his hair. "I can handle it from here. Go on down and put your stuff away."

"Is Beth coming to play with me tonight?"

"Yes, Beth's coming. Now scoot. I'll be down in a minute."

"'Kay." He made a dash for the door, stopping when his mother called him. It only took one look, the raised brow for him to remember. He looked back at Coop, flashed a quick, sunny grin. "Bye, mister."

The herd of elephants rampaged again, then there was the crash of a door slamming. "He makes an entrance," Zoe said as she turned back to Coop. "The dramatic flair comes from my mother. She's an actress, off-off-Broadway." Tilting her head, Zoe rested one bare foot on the bottom rung of the stepladder. "You look like you're ready to change your mind. You have a problem with children?"

"No." The kid might have thrown him off, but Coop doubted it would be a problem. The boy would hardly be beating a path to his door. And if he did, Coop thought, he could send him off again quickly enough. "No, he's, ah, cute."

"Yes, he is. I won't claim he's an angel, but he

won't make a nuisance of himself. If he gives you any trouble, just let me know."

"Sure. Look, I'll come by tomorrow to sign the lease and give you a check. I'll pick up the keys then."

"That'll be fine."

"Any special time good for you?"

She looked blank for a moment. "What's tomorrow?"

"Friday."

"Friday." She closed her eyes and flipped through her messy internal calendar. "I'm working between ten and two. I think." She opened her eyes again, smiled. "Yeah, I'm pretty sure. Anytime after two-thirty?"

"Fine. Nice meeting you, Mrs. Fleming."

She took his offered hand. "It's Miss," she said easily. "I'm not married. And since we'll be living together, so to speak, you can make it Zoe."

Chapter 2

No one answered the door. Again. Coop checked his watch and saw that it was quarter to three. He didn't like to think he was a man obsessed with time, but as his living centered around deadlines, he did respect it. There was no rusting station wagon in the driveway this time, but he walked around the back of the house, hoping. Before he could start up the stairs to the apartment, he was hailed from across the chain-link fence.

"Young man! Yoo-hoo, young man!" Across the yard next door came a flowered muumuu, topped with a curling thatch of brightly hennaed hair that crowned a wide face. The woman hurried to the fence in a whirl of color. It wasn't just the dress and the improbable hair, Coop noted. The face itself was a rainbow of rich red lipstick, pink cheeks and lavender eye shadow.

When she reached the fence, she pressed a many-ringed hand over the wide shelf of her breasts. "Not as young as I used to be," she said. "I'm Mrs. Finkleman."

"Hi."

"You're the young man who's going to live upstairs." Mrs. Finkleman, a born flirt, patted her curls. "Zoe didn't tell me you were so handsome. Single, are you?"

"Yeah," Coop said cautiously. "Miss Fleming was supposed to meet me. She doesn't seem to be home."

"Well, that's Zoe, flying here, flying there." Mrs. Finkleman beamed and leaned comfortably on the fence, as if she were settling in for a nice cozy gossip. "Got a dozen things on her plate at once, that girl does. Having to raise that sweet little boy all alone. Why, I don't know what I'd have done without my Harry when our young ones were coming up."

Coop was a reporter, after all. That, added to the fact that he was curious about his landlady, put him in interview mode. "The kid's father doesn't help out any?"

Mrs. Finkleman snorted. "Don't see hide nor hair of him. From what I'm told, he lit out the minute he found out Zoe was expecting. Left her high and dry, and her hardly more than a child herself. Far as I know, he's never so much as seen the boy. The little sweetheart."

Coop assumed she was referring to Keenan. "Nice kid. What's he, five, six?"

"Just four. Bright as a button. They grow them smarter these days. Teach them faster, too. The little love's in preschool now. He'll be home any minute."

"His mother went to pick him up, then?"

"Oh, no, not her week for car pool. Alice Miller—that's the white house with blue trim, down the block?—it's her week. She has a boy and a girl. Little darlings. The youngest, Steffie, is Keenan's age. Now her oldest, Brad, there's a pistol for you."

As she began to fill Coop in on the neighborhood rascal, he decided it was time to draw the interview to a close. "Maybe you could tell Miss Fleming I was by? I can leave a number where she can reach me when—"

"Oh, goodness." Mrs. Finkleman waved a hand. "I do run on. Nearly forgot why I came out here in the first place. Zoe called and asked me to look out for you. Got held up at the flower shop. She works there three days a week. That's Floral Bouquet, down in Ellicott City? Nice place, but expensive. Why, it's a crime to charge so much for a daisy."

"She got held up," Coop prompted.

"Her relief had car trouble, so Zoe's going to be a little late. Said you could go right on into the kitchen there, where she left the lease and the keys."

"That's fine. Thanks."

"No problem at all. This is a friendly neighborhood. Always somebody to lend a helping hand. I don't think Zoe mentioned what you did for a living."

"I'm a sportswriter for the *Dispatch.*"

"You don't say? Why, my Harry's just wild for sports. Can't budge him from in front of the TV when a game's on."

"That's what makes this country great."

Mrs. Finkleman laughed and gave Coop's arm an affectionate bat that might have felled a lesser man. "You men are all the same. You can come over and talk sports with Harry anytime. Me, if it's not baseball, it isn't worth talking about."

Coop, who'd been about to retreat, brightened. "You like baseball?"

"Son, I'm a Baltimore native." As if that said it all. "Our boys are going to go all the way this year. Mark my word."

"They could do it, if they heat those bats up. The pitching rotation's gold this year, and the infield's tight as a drum. What they need—"

Coop was interrupted by a cheerful toot. He glanced over to see Keenan burst out of a red sedan and rocket across the side yard.

"Hi, mister. Hi, Mrs. Finkleman. Carly Myers fell down, and there was blood." The big brown eyes gleamed wickedly. "Lots and lots of it, and she screamed and cried." He demonstrated, letting go with a piercing yell that had Coop's ears ringing. "Then she got a Band-Aid with stars on it." Keenan thought it would have been worth losing some blood for such a neat badge of honor. "Where's Mama?"

"Little lamb." Mrs. Finkleman leaned over the fence to pinch Keenan's cheek. "She's working a little late. She said you could come stay with me until she gets home."

"Okay." Keenan liked his visits next door, since they always included cookies and a rock on Mrs. Finkleman's wonderfully soft lap. "I gotta put my lunch box away."

"Such a good boy," Mrs. Finkleman cooed. "You come on over when you're done. Why don't you show the nice man inside so he can wait for your mother?"

"Okay."

Before Coop could take evasive action, his hand was clutched by Keenan's. He'd been right, he thought with a wince. It was sticky.

"We've got cookies," Keenan told him, cannily deducing that he could have double his afternoon's treat if he played his cards right.

"Great."

"We baked them ourselves, on our night off." Keenan sent Coop a hopeful look. "They're really good."

"I bet." Coop caught the back door before it could slam shut.

"There." Keenan pointed to a ceramic cookie jar in the shape of a big yellow bird on the counter. "In Big Bird."

"Okay, okay." Since it seemed like the best way to appease the kid, Coop reached in and pulled out a handful of cookies. When he dumped them on the table, Keenan's eyes went as wide as saucers. He could hardly believe his luck.

"You can have one, too." He stuffed an entire chocolate chip deluxe in his mouth and grinned.

"That good, huh?" With a shrug, Coop sampled one himself. The kid, Coop decided after the first bite, knew his cookies. "You'd better get next door."

Keenan devoured another cookie, stalling. "I gotta wash out my thermos, 'cause if you don't, it smells."

"Right." Cooper sat at the table to read through the lease while the boy dragged a stool in front of the sink.

Keenan squirted dishwashing liquid in the thermos, and then, when he noticed Coop wasn't paying any attention, he squirted some more. And more. He turned the water up high and giggled when soap began to bubble and spew. With his tongue caught between his teeth, he jiggled the stopper into the sink and began to play dishwasher.

Coop forgot about him, reading quickly. The lease seemed standard enough, he decided. Zoe had already signed both copies. He dashed his signature across from hers, folded his copy, then set the check he'd already written on the table. He'd picked up the keys and rose to tuck his copy in his pocket when he spotted Keenan.

"Oh, God."

The boy was drenched, head to foot. Soap bubbles dotted his face and hair. A good-sized puddle was forming on the tile at the base of the stool.

"What are you doing?"

Keenan looked over his shoulder, smiled innocently. "Nothing."

"Look, you've got water everywhere." Coop looked around for a towel.

"Everywhere," Keenan agreed, and, testing the opposition, he slapped his hands in the sink. Water and suds geysered.

"Cut it out! Jeez! Aren't you supposed to be somewhere else?" He grabbed a dish towel and advanced, only to be slapped in the face by the next geyser. His eyes narrowed. "Look, kid—"

He heard the front door slam. Like mother, like son, he thought.

"Keenan?" Zoe called out. "I hope you haven't been into those cookies."

Coop looked at the crumbs on the table, on the floor, floating in the soapy water.

"Oh, hell," he muttered.

"Oh, hell," Keenan echoed, beaming at him. He giggled and danced on his stool. "Hi, Mom."

Zoe, her arms full of day-old irises, took in the scene with one glance. Her son was as wet as a drowned dog, her kitchen looked as though a small hurricane had blown through. Hurricane Keenan, she thought. And her new tenant looked damp, frazzled, and charmingly sheepish.

Like a boy caught with his hand in the cookie jar, she noted, glancing at the telltale crumbs.

"Been playing dishwasher again?" With a calm that baffled Coop, she set the flowers down. "I'm just not sure it's the right career choice, Keen-man."

Keenan fluttered his long, wet lashes. "He wanted cookies."

Coop started to defend himself, then simply scowled at the boy.

"I'm sure he did. Go on into the laundry room and get out of those wet clothes."

"Okay." He jumped from the stool, splashing more water before he zoomed away. He stopped only long enough to give his mother a wet kiss before he disappeared into an adjoining room.

"Sorry I'm late," Zoe said easily, yanking the stopper out of the sink then walking to a cupboard to get a vase.

Coop opened his mouth. He started to explain what had gone on in the past ten minutes, but realized he wasn't at all sure. "I signed the lease."

"I see that. Would you mind putting some water in this?" She held out the vase. "I need to get a mop."

"Sure."

She was probably going to wallop the kid with it, Coop thought, and felt a quick tug of regret and guilt. But the sounds from the laundry room where she'd disappeared weren't those he associated with corporal punishment. They were a young boy's giggles, a woman's lusty laugh. Coop stood, a vase of water in his hands, and wondered at it.

"You're standing in a puddle," Zoe commented when she came back with a mop and pail.

"Oh, right." Coop glanced down at his wet high-tops, shifted. "Here's your vase."

"Thanks." She tended to her flowers first. "You met Mrs. Finkleman, I hear."

"News travels fast."

"Around here it does." When she handed him a dishcloth to dry his face with, he caught her scent—much more potent, much more colorful, than the flowers. She was wearing jeans and a baggy T-shirt with Floral Bouquet across the chest. Her hair, he noted, was some elusive shade between brown and blond. She wore it tied back in a jaunty ponytail.

When she lifted her brows, he realized he'd been staring. "Sorry. I mean—I'm sorry about the mess."

"Were you playing dishwasher, too?"

"Not exactly." It was impossible not to smile back, to ignore the quick pull of attraction.

It wouldn't be so bad, he mused, having a pretty

landlady, sharing the house with her, maybe an occasional meal. Or an occasional—

"Mama!" Keenan stood in the doorway, wearing nothing but skin. "I can't find my pants."

"In the basket by the washing machine," she told him, without taking her eyes from Coop's.

He'd forgotten about the kid, let himself fantasize a little before remembering she didn't come as a single. He took a long mental step backward and jingled the keys to his new apartment.

"I've got some boxes out in the car," he told her. "I'm going to move some things in this afternoon."

"That's fine." It was silly to feel disappointed, Zoe thought. Foolish to have felt that fast feminine flutter when she recognized interest in his eyes. More foolish to feel let down because the interest had blanked out when her child called her. "Do you need any help?"

"No, I can handle it. I've got a game to cover tonight, so I'm going to move the rest in tomorrow." He backed toward the door. "Thanks."

"Welcome aboard, Mr. McKinnon."

"Coop," he said as he stepped outside. "It's Coop."

Coop, she thought, leaning on the mop handle. It had seemed like such a good idea to make use of the apartment upstairs. The extra income would take some of the pressure off, and maybe add a few bonuses. Like that trip to Disney World that Keenan wanted so badly.

It had been a risk to buy the house, but she'd wanted her son to grow up in a nice neighborhood, with a yard, maybe a dog when he was a little older. The rental income would take away some of the risk.

But she hadn't realized it could add another, more personal risk. She hadn't realized how awkward it might be to have a tenant who was male, single, and absolutely gorgeous.

She laughed at herself. Dream on, Zoe, she thought. J. Cooper McKinnon was just like the rest, who ran like a hound when they heard the patter of little feet.

Something crashed in the laundry room. She just shook her head.

"Come on, sailor," she called to Keenan. "It's time to swab the deck."

Chapter 3

"Pretty good digs, Coop. Really, pretty good." Ben Robbins, a staff reporter for the *Dispatch,* sipped a cold one while surveying Coop's apartment. "I didn't think much of it when we hauled all your junk up here, but it ain't half-bad."

It was a lot better than not half-bad, and Coop knew it. He had everything exactly where he wanted it. The living room was dominated by his long, low-slung sofa of burgundy leather and his big-screen television, so perfect for viewing games. A couple of brass lamps, a nicely worn coffee table scuffed from the heels of the dozens of shoes that had rested on it and a single generous chair completed the formal section of the room.

There was an indoor basketball hoop, small-scaled, for practice—and because shooting a little round ball helped him think. A used pinball machine called Home Run, a stand that held two baseball bats, his tennis racket and a hockey stick, a pair of old boxing gloves hanging on the wall and a scarred Fooz Ball table made up the recreation area.

Coop wouldn't have called them toys. They were tools.

He'd chosen blinds, rather than curtains, for the windows. Blinds, he thought, that would close out the light if a man decided to treat himself to an afternoon nap.

The bedroom held little other than his bed, a nightstand and another TV. The room was for sleeping—or, if he got lucky, another type of sport.

But it was his office that pleased him most. He could already imagine himself spending hours there at his computer, a game playing on his desktop TV. He'd outfitted it with a big swivel chair, a desk that had just the right number of scars and burns, a fax, a dual-line phone and a VCR—to play back those controversial calls or heart-stopping plays.

With all the plaques and photos and sports memorabilia scattered about, it was home.

His home.

"Looks like the neighborhood bar," Ben said, and stretched out his short, hairy legs. "Where the jocks hang out."

Coop considered that the highest of compliments. "It suits me."

"To the ground," Ben agreed, and toasted Coop with his bottle of beer. "A place where a man can relax, be himself. You know, since I started living with Sheila, I've got little china things all over, and underwear hanging in the bathroom. The other day she comes home with a new bedspread. It's got *flowers* all over. Pink flowers." He winced as he drank. "It's like sleeping in a meadow."

"Hey." With all the smug righteousness of the unencumbered, Coop propped his feet on the coffee table. "Your choice, pal."

"Yeah, yeah. Too bad I'm nuts about her. And her an Oakland fan, too."

"Takes all kinds. Talk is the A's are trading Remirez."

Ben snorted. "Yeah, yeah, pull the other one, champ."

"That's the buzz." Coop shrugged, took a pull on his own beer. "Sending him to K.C. for Dunbar, and that rookie fielder, Jackson."

"They got to be crazy. Remirez hit .280 last season."

".285," Coop told him. "With twenty-four baggers. Led the team in errors, too."

"Yeah, but with a bat like that… And Dunbar, what's he? Maybe he hit .220?"

"It was .218, but he's like a vacuum cleaner at second. Nothing gets by him. And the kid's got potential. Big, strapping farm boy with an arm like a bullet. They need new blood. Most of the starting lineup's over thirty."

They argued baseball and finished their beers in complete male harmony.

"I've got a game to cover."

"Tonight? I thought the O's were in Chicago until tomorrow."

"They are." Coop pocketed his tape recorder, his pad, a pencil. "I'm covering the college game. There's a hot third baseman who's got the scouts drooling. Thought I'd take a look, cop an interview."

"What a job." Ben hauled himself to his feet. "Going to games, hanging around locker rooms."

"Yeah, it's a rough life." He slung an arm over Ben's shoulders as they headed out. "So, how's the story on neutering pets going?"

"Stuff it, Coop."

"Hey, some of us hang around the pound, some of us hang around the ballpark."

And a hell of a day it was for it, too, Coop thought. Balmy and clear-skied. He could almost smell roasting peanuts and hot dogs.

"While you're hanging around a bunch of sweaty college boys in jockstraps, I'll be snuggled up with a woman."

"Under a flowered bedspread."

"Yeah, but she says flowers make her feel sexy. And I'm here to tell you— My, oh, my..."

When Ben's small, square face went lax, Coop turned. He felt his own jaw drop. And, if he wasn't mistaken, his tongue landed on his shoes.

She was wearing what had to be the shortest skirt ever devised by man. Beneath it were a pair of endless legs that were molded into black fishnet hose. She swayed when she walked. How could she help it, when she stood in black skyscraper heels?

A tiny white bustier exposed a delicious amount of cleavage. Around her neck was a shiny black bow tie that, for reasons utterly inexplicable to Coop, made every male cell in his body sizzle.

Her hair was down, falling straight as a pin to her shoulders in a melding of tones that made him think of wild deer leaping through a sunlit forest.

She stopped, smiled, said something, but his mind had checked out the moment his eyes landed on her legs.

"...if you've settled in okay."

"Ah..." He blinked like a man coming out of a coma. "What?"

"I said I haven't had a chance to check and see if you've settled in okay."

"Fine." He folded his tongue back in his mouth and got a grip on himself. "Just fine."

"Good. Keenan came down with a cold, so things have been hectic. I caught a glimpse of you hauling things up the steps a couple of days ago."

"Hauling," he repeated. "Yeah. Ben," he said when his friend jabbed him. "This is Ben. He's been giving me a hand moving."

"Hi, Ben. I'm Zoe."

"Hi, Zoe," Ben said stupidly. "I'm Ben."

She just smiled. It was the outfit, she knew. As much as she hated it, she couldn't help but be amused by how it affected certain members of the species. "Do you work at the paper, too?"

"Yeah, I'm, ah, doing a story on neutering pets."

"Really?" She almost felt sorry for him, the way his Adam's apple was bobbing. "I'll be sure to look for it. I'm glad you're settling in okay. I've got to get to work."

"You're going out?" Coop said. "In that?"

Her lips twitched. "Well, this is my usual outfit when I'm carpooling, but I thought I'd wear it to work tonight. At Shadows? I'm a waitress. Nice meeting you, Ben."

She walked to her car. No, Coop thought, swayed to it, in those long, lazy strides. They were both still staring when she pulled out of the drive and cruised down the street.

"Your landlady," Ben said in a reverential whisper. "That was your landlady."

"I think it was." She hadn't looked like that when he signed the lease. Beautiful, yes—she'd been beautiful, but in a wholesome, unthreatening sort of way. She hadn't looked so...so... Words failed him. She was a mother, for God's sake, he reminded himself. She wasn't supposed to look like that. "She's got a kid."

"Yeah? What kind?"

"Human, I think."

"Come on."

"A boy," Coop said absently. "This high." He held a hand, palm down, about three feet from the ground.

"She may have a kid, but she's also got legs. This high." Ben waved a hand in front of his own throat. "You got a charmed life, Coop. My landlord's got arms like cinder blocks, and a tattoo of a lizard. You got one who looks like a centerfold."

"She's a mother," Coop said under his breath.

"Well, I wouldn't mind coming home to her for milk and cookies. See you at the sweatshop."

"Sure." Coop stood where he was, frowning at the quiet street. Mothers weren't supposed to look like that, he thought again. They were supposed to look...motherly. Safe. Comfortable. He blew out a breath, willed away the knot in his stomach.

She wasn't *his* mother, he reminded himself.

By midnight, Zoe's feet were screaming. Her back ached, and her arms felt as though she'd been hauling boulders rather than drink trays. She'd deflected six propositions, two of them good-hearted enough to amuse, one of them insulting enough to earn the gentleman in question a bruised instep, courtesy of one of her stiletto heels. The others had been the usual, and easily ignored.

It went with the territory, and it didn't bother her overmuch.

The lounge earned its name from the shadowy effect of neon and all the dim corners. The decor was fifties tacky, and the waitresses were dolled up like old-fashioned mindless floozies to match.

But the tips were excellent, and the clientele, for the most part, harmless.

"Two house wines, white, a Black Russian and a coffee, light." After calling out her order to the bartender, Zoe took a moment to roll her shoulders.

She hoped Beth had gotten Keenan to bed without any fuss. He'd been cranky all day—which meant he was nearly over his sniffles. He'd put up quite a fuss that morning, Zoe remembered, when she'd nixed the idea of him going to school.

Didn't get that from me, she thought. She'd never fussed about not going to school. Now, at twenty-five, she deeply regretted letting her education slide. If she'd applied herself, tried for college, she could have developed a skill, had a career.

Instead, she had a high school diploma she'd barely earned, and was qualified for little more than serving drinks to men whose eyes tried to crawl down her cleavage.

But she wasn't one for regrets. She'd done what she'd done, and she had the greatest prize of all. Keenan. In a couple of years, she figured, she'd have saved enough that she could turn in her bustier and take a night course. Once she had a few business courses under her belt, she could open her own flower shop. And she wouldn't have to leave Keenan with sitters at night.

She served her drinks, took an order from another table and thanked God her break was coming up in five minutes.

When she saw Coop walk in, her first thought was Keenan. But the sick alarm passed almost as quickly as it had come. Coop was relaxed, obviously scoping the place out. When his eyes met hers, he nodded easily and made his way through the scattered tables.

"I thought I'd stop in for a drink."

"This is the place for it. Do you want to sit at the bar, or do you want a table?"

"A table. Got a minute?"

"At quarter after I've got fifteen of them. Why?"

"I'd like to talk to you."

"Okay. What can I get you?"

"Coffee, black."

''Coffee, black. Have a seat.''

He watched her head toward the bar and tried not to dwell on how attractive she looked walking away. He hadn't come in because he wanted a drink, but because she seemed like a nice woman in a tight skirt—spot, he corrected. A tight spot.

Get hold of yourself, Coop, he warned himself. He knew better than to let a pair of long legs cloud his judgment. He'd only come in to ask a few questions, get the full story. That was what he did, and he was good at it. Just as he was good at dissecting a game, any game, and finding those small triumphs and small mistakes that influenced the outcome.

''We've been busy tonight.'' Zoe set two coffees on the table before sliding onto a chair across from Coop. She let out a long, heartfelt sigh, then smiled. ''This is the first time I've been off my feet in four hours.''

''I thought you worked in a flower shop.''

''I do, three days a week.'' She slid her cramped feet out of her shoes. ''Around Mother's Day, Christmas, Easter—you know, the big flower days, I can squeeze in more.'' She sipped the coffee she'd loaded with sugar and let it pump into her system. ''It's just a small shop, and Fred—that's the owner—only keeps on a couple of part-timers. That way he doesn't have to pay any of the bennies, like hospitalization, sick leave.''

''That's lousy.''

"Hey, it's a job. I like it. It's just Fred and Martha—she's his wife. They've taught me a lot about flowers and plants."

Someone pumped quarters into the juke. The room heated up with music. Coop leaned over the table so that she could hear him. For a moment he lost the thread somewhere in her big brown eyes.

"Have I met you somewhere before?" he asked her.

"In the apartment."

"No, I mean..." He shook his head, let it go. "Uh, why here?"

"Why here what?"

"Why do you work here?"

She blinked, those long lashes fluttering down, then up. "For a paycheck."

"It doesn't seem like you should be working in a bar."

"Excuse me?" Zoe wasn't sure if she should be amused or insulted. She chose the former simply because it was her nature. "Do you have a problem with cocktail waitresses?"

"No, no. It's just that, you're a mother."

"Yes, I am. I have a son to prove it." She laughed and leaned her chin on her fist. "Are you thinking it would be more appropriate for me to be home baking cookies or knitting a scarf?"

"No." Though it embarrassed him that he did. "It's that outfit," he blurted out. "And the way all these men look at you."

"If a woman's going to wear something like this, men are going to look. Looking's all they do," she added. "If it makes you feel better, I don't dress like this for PTA meetings."

He was feeling more ridiculous every second. "Look, it's none of my business. I just have a habit of asking questions. Seems to me you could do better than this. I mean, you've got the flower job, and the rent—"

"And I have a mortgage, a son who seems to outgrow his clothes and shoes every other week, a car payment, grocery bills, doctor bills."

"Doctor? Is the kid sick?"

Zoe rolled her eyes. Just when she was starting to get irritated, he deflated her. "No. Kids Keenan's age are always bringing some germ or other home from school. He needs regular checkups with his pediatrician, with the dentist. Those things aren't free."

"No, but there are programs. Assistance." He stopped, because those big brown eyes had turned fierce.

"I'm perfectly capable of earning a living, and of taking care of my child."

"I didn't mean—"

"Maybe I don't have a college degree or any fancy skills, but I can pay my own way, and my son doesn't lack for anything." She jammed her feet into the backbreaking heels and stood. "We've been doing just fine on our own, and I don't need some nosy jock reporter coming in here and telling me how to be a mother. Coffee's on the house, you jerk."

He winced as she stormed away from the table, then let out a long breath. Handled that one *real* well, Coop.

He wondered if there would be an eviction notice on his door in the morning.

Chapter 4

She didn't kick him out. She had thought of it, but had decided the satisfaction she'd gain didn't quite equal the rental income. Besides, she'd heard it all before.

One of the reasons she'd moved from New York was that she'd grown impossibly weary of friends and family telling her how to run her life. How to raise her son.

Baltimore had been a clean slate.

She'd had enough money put aside to afford a nice two-bedroom apartment and invest the rest. And because she was willing to work at any job, and work hard, she'd rarely been unemployed. It had been difficult for her to put Keenan in day-care. But he'd thrived. He had his mother's knack for making friends.

Now, two years after the move, she had a house, and a yard, in the kind of neighborhood she wanted for her son. And she'd paid for every bit of it on her own.

Too many people had told her she was crazy, that she was too young, that she was throwing her life and her chances away. With a grunt, Zoe shoved the lawn mower around and began to cut another strip of grass. *Her* grass, she thought with clenched teeth.

She'd proved them wrong. She'd had her baby, kept her baby, and she was making a decent life for him. She and Keenan weren't statistics. They were a family.

They didn't need anyone to feel sorry for them, or to offer handouts. She was taking care of everything, one step at a time. And she had plans. Good, solid plans.

The tap on her shoulder made her jump. When she whipped her head around and looked at Coop, her hands tightened on the mower. "What?"

"I want to apologize," he shouted. When she only continued to glare at him, he reached down and shut off the engine. "I want to apologize," he repeated. "I was out of line last night."

"Really?"

"I'm sort of addicted to poking into other people's business."

"Maybe you should go cold turkey." She reached down to grab the pull cord. His hand closed over hers.

She stared at it a moment. He had big hands, rough-palmed. She remembered the impression she'd gotten of strength and energy. Now the hand was gentle and hard to resist.

She hadn't felt a man's hands—hadn't wanted to feel a man's hands—in a very long time.

"Sometimes I push the wrong buttons," Coop continued. He was staring at their hands, as well, thinking how small hers felt under his. How soft. "It's earned me a fist in the face a time or two." He tried a smile when her gaze slid up to his.

"That doesn't surprise me."

She didn't smile back, but he sensed a softening. The roar of the mower had awakened him. When he'd looked out and seen her marching along behind it in baggy shorts, a T-shirt and a ridiculous straw hat, he'd wanted to go back to bed. But he'd been compelled to seek her out.

It was only a flag of truce, he told himself. After all, he had to live with her. More or less.

"I didn't mean to be critical. I was curious about you. And the kid," he added quickly. "And maybe seeing you in that outfit last night pushed a few of my buttons."

She lifted a brow. That was honest enough, she thought. "All right. No permanent damage."

It had been easier than he'd expected. Coop decided to press his luck. "Listen, I've got to cover the game this afternoon. Maybe you'd like to come along. It's a nice day for baseball."

She supposed it was. It was warm and sunny, with a nice, freshening breeze. There were worse ways to spend the day than in a ballpark with an attractive man who was doing his best to pry his foot out of his mouth.

"It sounds like fun—if I didn't have to work. But Keenan would love it." She watched his jaw drop, and smothered a smile.

"Keenan? You want me to take him?"

"I can't think of anything he'd rather do. Some of the kids play in their yards, and they let him chase the ball. But he's never seen the real thing, except on TV." She smiled now, guilelessly, and held back a hoot of laughter. She could all but see Coop's mind working.

"I don't know too much about kids," he said, backpedaling cautiously.

"But you know about sports. It'll be great for Keenan to experience his first real game with an expert. When are you leaving?"

"Ah…a couple of hours."

"I'll make sure he's ready. This is awfully nice of you." While he stood staring, she leaned over and kissed his cheek. After one hard tug, she had the mower roaring again.

Coop stood planted like a tree when she strolled away. What the hell was he supposed to do with a kid all afternoon?

He bought popcorn, hot dogs and enormous cups of soft drinks. Coop figured food would keep the kid quiet. Keenan had bounced on the seat of the car throughout the drive to Camden Yards, and since they had arrived he'd goggled at everything.

Coop had heard "What's that?" and "How come?" too many times to count. Nervous as a cat, he settled into the press box with his laptop.

"You can watch through the window here," he instructed Keenan. "And you can't bother anybody, because they're working."

"Okay." Almost bursting with excitement, Keenan clutched his hot dog.

There were lots of people in the press box, some with neat computers, like Coop, others with headphones. A few of them had smiled at him, and all of them had said hello to Coop. Keenan knew Coop was important. As his mother had instructed, he kept close and didn't ask for any presents. Even though there had been really neat stuff at the stands. His mother had given him five whole dollars and told him he could buy a souvenir. But there'd been so many he didn't know which to pick. And Coop had walked so fast he'd hardly been able to look.

But it didn't matter, because he was at a real ball game.

Wide-eyed, he stared down at the field. It was bigger than anything he'd imagined. He knew where the pitcher would stand, and he recognized home plate, but he wasn't sure of anything else.

The big scoreboard exploded with pictures, and words he couldn't read. Circling it all were the stands, filled with more people than he'd ever seen.

When they announced the lineup, he looked down at the players with naked admiration. The national anthem began, and, recognizing it, Keenan stood up, as he'd been taught.

Coop glanced over, saw the boy standing, with a hot dog in one hand and a big, dazzling grin on his face. Suddenly he remembered his first time at a ballpark. His eager hand gripping his father's, his eyes trying to see everything at once, and his heart so full of the excitement, of the game, of just being a boy.

As the players took the field, Coop reached over and tugged on Keenan's bright hair. ''Pretty cool, huh?''

''It's the best ever. Those are our guys, right?''

''Those are our guys. They're gonna kick butt.''

Keenan giggled and leaned closer to the glass to watch the first pitch. ''Kick butt,'' he said with relish.

He didn't, as Coop had expected, fidget, whine or make a general nuisance of himself. Because he was accustomed to working under noisy and confusing conditions, Keenan's constant questions didn't annoy him overmuch. At least, he thought, the kid had the good sense to ask.

Between innings, Keenan peered over Coop's shoulder and sounded out the words that were popping up on the computer screen, and he did transfer some mustard from his hands onto Coop's sleeve. But it wasn't the disaster Coop had envisioned.

Coop even felt a quick tug of pride when the play-by-play announcer called Keenan over and let the boy sit in his lap for an inning.

Most kids would've been running around the booth begging for more candy. But this one, Coop thought, had come for the game.

"How come he didn't run all the way? How come he didn't?" Keenan shifted from foot to foot. His bladder was past full, but he couldn't bear to miss a minute.

"The throw went to second, so he was forced out," Coop explained. "See, the second baseman caught the ball and stepped on the bag to retire the side."

"Retire the side," Keenan repeated reverently. "But we're still winning?"

"The O's are up by one going into the top of the ninth. Looking at the batting order, I'd say they'll put in a southpaw."

"Southpaw," Keenan repeated, as if it were gospel.

"A left-handed reliever. Probably Scully." He glanced over and noted that Keenan was holding his crotch. "Uh, got a problem?"

"Nuh-uh."

"Let's hit the john—the bathroom." He took Keenan's hand and hoped it wasn't too late. As they passed through the door, Scully was announced as the relief.

"Just like you said." Keenan looked up at Coop with dazzling admiration. "You're smarter than anybody."

Coop felt a grin break out over his face. "Let's just say I know the game."

When they arrived home, Keenan was wearing a new Orioles jersey and carrying an autographed baseball in a pint-size baseball glove. He waved a pennant in his other hand as he scrambled up the steps.

"Look! Look what Coop got me!" He barreled into his mother who'd barely walked in the door herself. "We went into the locker room with the real Orioles, and they signed the baseball for me. To keep."

"Let's see." She took the ball and examined it. "This is really special, Keenan."

"I'm gonna keep it forever. And I got this shirt, too, like they wear. And a glove. It even fits."

Emotion backed up in her throat. "It certainly does. Looks like you're all ready to play ball."

"I'm gonna play third base, 'cause it's the...the..."

"Hot corner," Coop supplied.

"Yeah. Can I go show Mr. Finkleman? Can I show him my baseball?"

"Sure."

"He's gonna be surprised." He turned and threw his arms around Coop's legs. "Thanks, thanks for taking me. I liked it best of anything. Can we go again, and take Mama?"

"Uh, yeah, I guess. Sure." Feeling awkward again, he patted Keenan's head.

"Okay!" Giving Coop one last squeeze, Keenan raced out the door to show off his treasures.

"You didn't have to buy him all that stuff," Zoe began. "Taking him was enough."

"No big deal. He didn't ask for it, or anything." Coop stuck his hands in his pockets. "He got such a charge out of meeting the players, and one thing kind of led to another."

"I know. I hear our team won."

"Yeah. Clipped them by one. I had to stop by the paper and file the story, or we'd have been here sooner."

"I just got in myself." On impulse, she walked over, wrapped her arms around him and hugged. Coop's hands stayed paralyzed in his pockets. "I owe you. You gave him a great day. He won't forget it." She drew back. "Neither will I."

"It's no big deal. He just hung out in the press box."

"It's a very big deal, especially since I trapped you into it." She laughed and tossed back her hair. "You were so transparent this morning, Coop. The idea of having a four-year-old tagging along terrified you. But you did good, real good. Anyway— Sorry,'' she said when the phone rang. ''Hello? Oh, hi, Stan. Tonight? I'm not scheduled.'' Letting out a breath, she sat on the arm of a chair. ''I'll have to let you know. No, Stan, I can't tell you now. I have to see if I can find a sitter. An hour, then. Yes, I understand you're in a jam. I'll call you back.''

''Problem?''

''Hmmm... Two of the waitresses called in sick for tonight. They're short-staffed.'' She was already dialing the phone. ''Hi, Mrs. Finkleman. Yeah, I know. He had a great time. Mm-hmm...'' Zoe's gaze flicked up to Coop as Mrs. Finkleman told her how important it was for a boy to have a man in his life. ''I'm sure you're right. I was wondering if you're busy tonight. Oh. That's right, I forgot. No, it's nothing. Have a good time.''

Zoe hung up and pursed her lips. ''It's their bingo night,'' she told Coop. ''Beth's got a date. Maybe Alice.'' She reached for the phone again, shook her head. ''No, she's having her in-laws over for dinner.'' Her eyes lit on Coop and narrowed in speculation. ''You didn't have any problem with Keenan today.''

''No,'' Coop said slowly, wary of another trap. ''He was cool.''

''Stan doesn't need me in until nine. Keenan goes

to bed at eight, so you wouldn't have to do anything but hang around, watch television or whatever."

"Hang around here, while you work?" He took a step back. "Just me and the kid—like a baby-sitter? Listen..."

"I'll pay you. Beth gets two an hour, but I can up the ante."

"I don't want your money, Zoe."

"That's so sweet." She smiled, took his hand and squeezed. "Really, so sweet of you. If you could come down about eight-thirty."

"I never said—"

"You can help yourself to anything in the kitchen. I'll make some brownies, if I have time. I'd better call Stan back before he pulls out what's left of his hair." She picked up the phone, beamed at Coop. "Now I owe you two."

"Yeah, right." He hurried out before she could find some way to owe him three.

Chapter 5

For the next couple of hours, Coop immersed himself in ''All in the Game,'' his weekly syndicated column. The kid had given him the hook, he thought. The first visit to a ball game, the passing on of tradition, and the bond that was forged over the cheers, the crack of the bat, the peanut shells.

It was a good piece, Coop decided, and wrote easily. He supposed since he owed the idea to Keenan the least he could do was hang around downstairs and eat brownies while the kid slept.

He wandered back down just as Zoe came through the kitchen door.

She hadn't been sure he'd come. She knew she'd hustled him, and after she'd finished being amused by it, she felt guilty. But here he was, right on time, standing at the foot of the steps.

"I pushed you into a corner...." she began.

"Yeah, you did." She looked so somber, he had to smile. "You've got a real talent for it."

She shrugged her shoulders and smiled back at him. "Sometimes being pushy's the only way to get things done, but I always feel bad about it after. I did bake brownies."

"I could smell them all the way upstairs." When she didn't move, he tilted his head. Funny, though she was wearing that sexy waitress rig again, she didn't seem so outrageous. Except for that bow tie, he thought. Something about that black tie around that slim white throat shot straight to his libido.

"You going to let me in, or do you want me to stand out here?"

"I have this guilt thing," she explained, "whenever I have to ask anyone for a favor. And it was so sweet of you to take Keenan to the game, especially when..."

"When I'd been asking you out?"

She shrugged her shoulders again, let them fall. He was looking at her that way again, and something in her body was reacting helplessly. Better, she thought, to set the rules quickly. "I don't go out with men. I should have told you straight out."

He had to force himself not to lift a hand to that neat little bow and tug. "At all?"

"It's just easier not to. They're not interested in Keenan, or they pretend they are so they can talk me into bed." When he rocked back on his heels and cleared his throat, she laughed. "What they don't know is that they're clear as cellophane. You see, Keenan and I are a team. As a sportswriter, you should know what that means."

"Sure. I get it."

"Anyway, you gave him a really wonderful day, and I feel like I'm twisting your arm about tonight."

He decided, after a moment, that she wasn't doing it on purpose. There was just too much sincerity in that glorious face for a con. And if there was a twinge of guilt because he had given considerable thought to talking her into bed, that was his problem.

"Look, he's asleep, right?"

"Yes. All the excitement wore him out."

"So, I'll eat your brownies and watch your TV. No big deal."

Her smile came easily now, beautifully, and made his mouth water. "I left the number of the club by the phone, just in case. The Finklemans should be home by eleven. She'd come over and relieve you if you want."

"We'll play it by ear."

"Thanks, really." She stepped back into the kitchen to let him in. "My shift ends at two, at closing."

"Long day for you."

"I've got tomorrow off." After grabbing her purse, she took a quick look around. "Make yourself at home, okay?"

"I will. See you."

She hurried out, those incredibly sexy heels clicking across the tile. Coop let out a long breath and told himself to settle down. The lady had just set the ground rules. Fun and games were out.

She had the face of a siren, the body of a goddess, and legs designed to make a strong man whimper—but deep in her heart she was Betty Crocker.

Coop took a deep sniff and decided to content himself with a plate of double fudge brownies.

The storm rolled in just before midnight. Coop had taken Zoe at her word and made himself at home. He was stretched out on her couch, sunk deep in the cushions, with his feet propped comfortably on her coffee table. He was dozing in front of an old war movie, his only regret being that he hadn't thought to bring a couple of beers down with him.

Zoe's selection ran to milk, juice and some unidentified green liquid.

He'd poked around a little—it was simply in his nature. The clutter ran throughout the house, but he began to see a pattern to it. Obviously she wasn't a detail person, but the general lack of order made the house comfortable, even cozy. Coop wasn't sure if the result was by design or simply because she was a woman who worked two jobs and had a kid to raise.

And from the library books he'd found stacked here and there, it seemed she spent most of her free time reading up on flowers, car repair, tax laws and time management.

He couldn't help but think it was a waste of a perfectly stunning woman, this voluntary burial of self in books and nowhere part-time jobs.

But it wasn't his problem.

The crash of thunder from outside harmonized nicely with the artillery barrage on the TV screen. Coop had just decided that this baby-sitting racket was a snap.

Then he heard the wailing.

Marines didn't wail, he thought fuzzily, especially when they were battling Nazi scum. He yawned, circled his neck until it cracked, then spotted Keenan.

The boy stood at the base of the stairs in Batman pajamas, a battered stuffed dog clutched in one arm and tears pouring down his face.

"Mama!" His voice sharpened like an ice pick, then hitched. "Where's my mama?"

"She's at work." Coop straightened on the sofa and stared helplessly. "Something wrong?"

A flash of lightning lit the room. By the time the thunder rolled in answer, Keenan screamed like a banshee and launched himself into Coop's lap.

"I'm scared. There's monsters outside. They're coming to get me."

"Hey..." Coop gave the head buried in his chest an inadequate pat. "Hey, it's just a thunderstorm."

"Monsters," Keenan sobbed. "I want Mama."

"Well, she's—" He started to swear, caught himself. The poor kid was shaking. With an instinct he didn't recognize, Coop cuddled Keenan in his lap. "You don't like storms, huh?" All Keenan could do was shake his head and burrow deeper. "They're just like fireworks. You know, on the Fourth of July, or after your team wins the pennant? They probably just had a big game up there. They're celebrating."

"Monsters," Keenan repeated, but he'd calmed enough to lift his head and look at Coop. "Big black monsters with sharp teeth." He jolted at the next clap of thunder. Fresh tears started to roll. "They want to eat me."

"Nah." Experimentally, Coop tested Keenan's biceps. "You're too tough."

"I am?"

"You bet. Any monsters who looked in here would see you and run for their lives. They'd never take on Coop and the Keen-man."

Keenan sniffled, rubbed a fist over his eyes. "Really?"

"Absolutely." Coop saw Keenan's lower lip tremble when thunder grumbled. "Home run," he said, and Keenan's trembling mouth curved in a hesitant smile.

"Can I stay out here with you?"

"Sure. I guess."

Keenan, an expert in such matters, settled himself comfortably in Coop's lap, laid his head against Coop's heart and sighed.

Zoe was swaying with fatigue by the time she let herself in. It was nearly 3:00 a.m., and she'd been up and going for twenty hours straight. All she wanted was to fall facedown on her bed and sleep.

She saw them in the gray light of the snowy television screen. They were curled together on the couch, the boy snuggled deep against the man. Something shifted inside her at the sight of them, both sleeping deeply, Keenan's tousled golden hair beneath Coop's broad, tanned hand.

She set her purse and her keys aside without taking her eyes off them.

How small her son looked, and how safe.

She slipped out of her shoes and walked to them on stockinged feet. In a natural gesture, she brushed a hand over Coop's hair before gently lifting her son. Keenan stirred, then settled against her.

"Mama."

"Yes, baby," she murmured. She nuzzled him as she carried him away, caught the scent of man mixed with boy.

"The monsters came, but we scared them away."

"Of course you did."

"Coop said the thunder's just fireworks. I like fireworks."

"I know." She laid him in his bed, smoothing the sheets, his hair, kissing his soft cheeks. "Go back to sleep now."

But he already had. She watched him a moment longer in the faint glow of his night-light, then turned and went back downstairs to Coop.

He was sitting up now, his head in his hands, the heels rubbing against his eyes. She switched off the buzzing television set, then sat on the arm of the couch. Any man who could sleep so comfortably with a child, to her mind, had unlimited potential.

She wondered, just for an instant, what it would feel like to curl up beside him.

"The storm woke him?"

"Yeah." His voice was rusty. He cleared it. "He was pretty spooked."

"He said you chased the monsters away."

"Seemed like the right thing to do." He turned his head to look at her. Those big brown eyes were sleepy and smiling. The quick hitch in his heartbeat warned him to be on his way. But he lingered. "He's okay now?"

"He's fine. You'd make a good daddy."

"Oh, well..." That had him moving. He stood,

working out the kinks. ''That's not my line. But it was no big deal.''

''It was to me.'' She'd embarrassed him, she noted, and she hadn't meant to. ''Why don't I fix you breakfast tomorrow?''

''Huh?''

''Pay you back with pancakes. Mrs. Finkleman tells me you bring in a lot of pizza and Chinese, so I don't imagine you cook. Do you like pancakes?''

''Who doesn't?''

''Then let me know when you're up and around. I'll flip some for you.'' She lifted a hand, brushed the hair from his brow. ''Thanks for helping me out.''

''No problem.'' He took a step away, swore under his breath and turned back. ''Listen, I've just got to do this, okay?''

Before she could respond, he took her face in his hands and closed his mouth over hers.

The kiss was quick, and it was light, and it sent sparks snapping down her nerve ends.

When she didn't move a muscle, he lifted his head, looked at her. She was staring at him, her eyes heavy and dark. He thought he saw the same stunned reaction in them that was curling somewhere in his gut. She opened her mouth as if to speak, but he shook his head and kissed her again. Longer, deeper, until he felt her bones begin to melt. Until he heard the small whimper of pleasure purr in her throat.

Her hands slid up his arms, gripped, then moved up to tangle in his hair. They stood there, locked against each other.

One of them quivered, perhaps both. It didn't seem to matter as the warm taste of her seeped into his mouth, into his blood. It was like a dream that he hadn't yet shaken off, one that tempted him to sink back in, to forget reality.

She'd forgotten it. All she knew for one glorious moment was that she was being held in strong arms, that her mouth was being savored wonderfully, and that needs, so long dormant, were swimming to the surface and breaking into life.

Touch me. She wondered if she said it, or if the words simply whirled hazily in her head. But his hand, hard and sure, ran once down her body, kindling fires.

She remembered what it was to burn, and what it was like when the flames died out and left you alone.

"Coop." Oh, she wanted, so badly, just to let it happen. But she wasn't a young, reckless girl this time. And she had more to think of than herself. "Coop. No."

His mouth clung to hers for another moment, his teeth nipping. But he drew back. He was, he realized, as breathless as a man who'd slid headfirst into home plate.

"Now I'm supposed to say I'm sorry."

She shook her head. "No, you're not. I'm not."

"Good." The hands that were resting on her shoulders kneaded once, then slipped away into his pockets. "Me neither. I've been thinking about doing that since I first saw your feet."

Her brows rose. Surely she'd heard him wrong. "My what?"

"Your feet. You were standing on the ladder, painting. You weren't wearing any shoes. You've got tremendously sexy feet."

"Really?" It amazed her that he could tie her into helpless knots one minute, then make her laugh the next. "Thanks. I think."

"I guess I'd better go."

"Yeah, you'd better."

He nodded, started out. This time, when he stopped, she braced, and she yearned. But he simply turned and looked at her. "I'm not going to try to talk you into bed. But I want you there. I figured I should let you know."

"I appreciate it," she said in a shaky voice.

When the door closed behind him, she let her weak legs fold and sat down on the couch. What, she asked herself, was she supposed to do now?

Chapter 6

When Coop dragged himself out of bed, it was nearly noon. He stumbled into the shower and nearly drowned himself before both of his eyes opened. Wet and out of sorts, he rubbed himself down, gave a moment's thought to shaving, then dismissed the idea.

He tugged on gym shorts and a T-shirt before heading directly to the coffeemaker. While it brewed, he opened his front door and let the full power of the sun shock him the rest of the way awake.

They were in the yard, Zoe and Keenan, laughing as mother tried to help son hit fungoes with a plastic bat. The kid wasn't having much luck, Coop noted. But he was sure having fun. He started to step back inside before either of them spotted him. But the jock in him had him kibitzing.

"He'll never hit anything standing that way," Coop called out, and had two pair of big brown eyes looking up in his direction.

"Hi, Coop. Hi. I'm playing baseball." Thrilled to have an audience, Keenan waved his bat and nearly caught his mother on the chin.

"Watch it, champ," she said, and shifted out of range. "Good morning," she called out. "Want your breakfast?"

"Yeah, maybe."

Keenan took another pathetic swing and had Coop muttering under his breath. Swung like a girl. Somebody had to show the kid how to hold a bat, didn't they? he asked himself as he started down.

"You're choking it too much."

Zoe's brows drew together. "The book I got said—"

"Book." He cursed automatically. Keenan echoed him. "Sorry," he muttered when Zoe gave him a narrow-eyed look. "Now listen, you learn how to add and subtract from books. You don't learn baseball. Just like a girl." He crouched down and adjusted Keenan's hands.

Zoe had been ready to concede to the expert, but the last statement stopped her. "Excuse me? Are you implying that females can't play sports?"

"Not what I said. Swing from the shoulders," he told Keenan. Coop might have been grouchy, but he wasn't stupid. "There are plenty of terrific female athletes. Keep your eye on the ball, kid." He kept one hand around Keenan's and lightly tossed the ball up in the air with the other. The bat connected with a hollow thud.

"I hit it! I hit it really, really hard!"

"Major league stuff." Coop slid his eyes back up to Zoe's. "I thought you were making pancakes."

"I was— I am." She blew out a breath. "I guess you're taking over."

"Well, I don't know diddly about pancakes, and you don't know squat about baseball. Why don't we both do what we know?"

"Like it's a big deal to hit a stupid ball with a stupid bat," she muttered as she strode to the back door.

"You can't do it."

She stopped dead in her tracks, eyes narrowed, turned. "I certainly can."

"Yeah, right. Okay, Keenan, let's try it again."

"I believe it's my turn." Challenge in her every movement, Zoe slipped the bat from her son's hands.

"Are you going to hit it, Mama? Are you?"

"You bet I am." She held out a hand for the ball Coop was holding. She tossed it up, swung, and batted the ball to the chain-link fence bordering the side yard. Keenan let out a cheer and raced to retrieve it.

Coop sniffed, smiled. "Not bad, for a girl. But anybody can hit a fungo."

“Keenan’s too young for anything but a plastic ball.”

“No, a fungo’s when you toss it up yourself and hit it.”

“Oh.”

“I’m gonna throw it, Coop. You catch.”

“Sure, zip it in here.”

It took Keenan three tries, running in closer each time, to send the ball anywhere near Coop.

“I suppose you don’t think I could hit it if you threw it at me....” Zoe began.

“Pitch it to you,” Coop said patiently. “I would pitch it to you.”

“All right, pitch it to me, then.” She raised the bat.

“Fine, but you might want to turn a little more to the side. That’s it,” he said, backing away. “Zoe, you’re holding the bat like you’re going to use it to hammer a nail. Okay, here it comes.”

He tossed the ball soft and underhand, but she still had to grit her teeth to keep herself from jerking away. Because her pride and her son’s respect for women were at stake, she swung hard. No one was more stunned than Zoe when she connected. Coop snatched the ball an instant before it could smash his nose.

“Well.” Zoe handed the bat back to a wide-eyed Keenan, dusted her hands. “I’ll go see about those pancakes.”

“She hit it really hard,” Keenan said admiringly.

"Yeah." Coop watched the back door swing shut behind her. "Your mother's really...something, kid."

"Will you pitch to me, Coop? Will you?"

"Sure. But let's work on that stance, huh? You gotta look like a ballplayer."

When Zoe finished flipping the last pancake on the stack, she looked out the window and saw her son swing the bat. The ball didn't go far, but Coop made a pretense of a diving catch, missing, while Keenan danced gleefully in place.

"Too hot to handle," Coop claimed, and Keenan jumped on top of him. "Hey, there's no tackling in baseball. Football's out of season." He scooped the wriggling boy up and held him upside down. Somewhere along the line, his sour mood had vanished.

It became a habit to spend time with the boy. Nothing planned, just playing a little catch in the yard or showing Keenan how to dunk baskets in the apartment. It wasn't as though he were attached to the kid, Coop assured himself. But when he had some free time and the boy wanted to hang around, what was the harm? Maybe it was sort of nice to see those big eyes all full of hero worship. And maybe it wasn't so much of a hardship to listen to that rollicking belly laugh Keenan burst into when something struck his fancy.

If the boy sometimes came along with the bonus of his mother, it wasn't exactly a hardship.

The fact was, he had seen a great deal more of Keenan than Zoe since the night of the thunderstorm. She was friendly enough, but she'd been careful—or so it seemed to Coop—not to be alone with him.

That was something he was going to fix, he decided as he shut down his computer.

He grabbed a couple of miniature race cars, some of the flotsam and jetsam of boyhood that Keenan had left in his apartment. If Coop knew Zoe as he thought he was beginning to, the toys would be an easier entry than a bouquet of long-stemmed roses.

Jiggling the cars in his hand, he strode down the steps to knock on her kitchen door.

In the laundry room, Zoe slammed down the lid on the washer. "Who is it?"

"It's Coop."

She hesitated, started the machine. "Come on in. I'll be right out." She hefted a basket of clean laundry, as much out of defense as out of necessity, and went into the kitchen.

God, he looked good. She had really, really tried not to dwell on how good the man looked. So damn male, she thought, the rangy, athletic body, the muscles, the dark, untidy hair, and those wonderful pale green eyes. She wished her heart wouldn't always stutter when he aimed one of his cocky grins in her direction.

"Hi." She plopped the basket on the kitchen table

and immediately began busying her hands folding socks.

"Hi." The kitchen was cluttered, as always. She really needed someone to help her organize, he thought. God, she smelled fantastic. "Keenan left these upstairs." Coop set the cars on the table. "I thought he might be looking for them."

"Thanks."

"So where is he?"

"In school."

"Oh, right." Coop knew Keenan's schedule as well as he knew yesterday's box scores. "You just get in from the flower shop?"

"Mmm-hmm... Business is picking up. We've got a couple of weddings. Actually, I could work full-time for the next three weeks, but it just doesn't fit Keenan's schedule."

"What do you mean?" Idly he plucked a shirt from the basket.

"Well, the spring weddings. The arrangements take a lot of extra hands, so Fred asked if I could put in full days for a while."

"So, that's good, right?"

"The school Keenan goes to is really more of a preschool than day-care. It doesn't stay open after three. And I have the car pool next week, anyway. Plus, I promised to take him and some of the other kids swimming at the community center on Friday. He's really looking forward to it."

"Yeah, he mentioned it." About twenty times, Coop recalled.

"I don't want to let him down."

"So, I'll do it."

She looked back up, socks dangling from her hands. "What?"

He couldn't believe he'd said that. He stared at her for another moment, then shrugged. "I said I'd do it. It's no big deal. He can hang with me when he gets home from school."

She tilted her head. "Don't you have a job?"

"That's what I call it, since they pay me." He smiled, finding the idea went down easily. "I do most of my writing here, and he could tag along when I go in to the paper or on an interview. He'd probably get a kick out of it."

"I'm sure he would." She narrowed her eyes. Why couldn't she get a handle on J. Cooper McKinnon? "But why would you?"

He wasn't sure he had the answer to that, so he punted. "Why not? He's not that much of a pest."

With a laugh, she went back to her laundry. "Maybe he's not, but you forgot the car pool."

"I can drive. What's the big deal about hauling a bunch of kids to school and back?"

"I can't begin to tell you," she murmured. It was, perhaps, something every adult should experience for himself. "And the swimming."

"I was captain of the swim team in college. All-state."

She glanced up at that. "I thought you played baseball. Uh, Keenan mentioned it."

"Yeah, I did. Two hundred and twelve RBIs my last season. I played basketball, too, averaged forty-two points a game." He was bragging, Coop realized. Like some gawky teenager trying to impress the head cheerleader. He frowned down at the little cars, began to slide one over the table.

"Keenan says you make great engine noises."

"Yeah, it's a talent."

He'd embarrassed himself, Zoe realized, and she wanted to hug him. "Tell you what. Why don't we take it a day at a time? If you decide you can't handle it—"

His eyes flashed up at that. "I think I can handle one scrawny kid and a few of his pals."

"Okay. If you decide you don't *want* to handle it, no hard feelings."

"Fine. When do you want to start?"

"Tomorrow would be great."

"Okay." That was settled. Now, he thought, it was on to other business. "How about dinner?"

Her eyes widened in surprise. "Um…sure. We're just going to have chicken. I'll probably fry it."

"No." He stepped closer. She stepped back. "I mean, why don't we have dinner? Out. You and me."

"Oh, well..." Good answer, she thought foolishly. Very succinct. She took another step in retreat. "I have to work tonight."

"Tomorrow."

"I don't really go out."

"I've noticed. What are you backing away from, Zoe?"

"You." Annoyed with herself, she held up a hand. And found it pressed against his chest. "I don't want to date anyone. Start anything. I have very good reasons."

"You'll have to tell me about them sometime." He reached up, combed a hand through her hair and loosened the band that held it back.

"You're not going to kiss me again."

"Sure I am." He touched his lips to hers to prove it. His eyes remained open as he drew her lower lip into his mouth, as he used his tongue, his teeth, to tease and seduce. "You've got an incredible mouth."

She couldn't get her breath. Even as she gasped for it, her vision dimmed. It was all she wanted. It seemed her life depended on keeping her lips against his. This wasn't fair, she thought dimly as she began to sink into the glory of sensation. Too long, she told herself. Surely she was reacting this way only because it had been so terribly long since she'd allowed herself to feel only as a woman.

She was melting against him like wax. He hadn't

known how painfully erotic it would be to feel that long, lean body go fluid. He'd only meant to kiss her, to test them both, but his hands were already reaching, stroking, exploring.

His touch, those hard, callused hands against her bare skin, all but brought her to her knees.

"I have to think."

"Think later." He pressed his mouth to her throat.

Oh, it was glorious, glorious to ache again. But she knew too well what came from soothing that ache. "Coop, we can't do this."

"Yes, we can. I'll show you."

With a laugh that came out half moan, she turned her head away. "My head's spinning. You have to stop. God, do you have any idea what you're doing to me?"

"I haven't even started. Come upstairs, come upstairs with me, Zoe. I want to feel you under me. I want to feel myself inside you."

"I want to." She trembled, the needs exploding inside her like firebombs. "Coop, I need to think first. I have to think. I haven't been with anyone in five years."

His mouth stopped its desperate journey over her throat. Slowly he drew back to look at her. Her eyes were clouded, and her mouth was swollen and ripe. "No one?"

"No." She swallowed and prayed for her system to

level before she gave in to the urge to rip off his clothes and cut loose. ''Since before Keenan was born. I feel like all those needs dried up—like old leaves. You've set a match to them, and I don't know how to handle it.''

''The kid's father,'' Coop said carefully. ''You're still in love with him.''

''No.'' She might have laughed at that, if she weren't so shaken. ''He has nothing to do with it. Well, of course he does, but… I have to sit down.'' She walked unsteadily to a chair. ''I knew this was going to happen. I think I knew it the first time I saw you. There's been no one, because I didn't want anyone. Because Keenan was all that mattered to me. I have plans.'' That came out as an accusation, and her eyes darkened. ''Damn it, I have plans. I want to go back to school. I want to have my own flower shop one day.'' Her voice began to catch, alarming him.

''Zoe—''

But she barreled right over him. ''And everything was going along fine. I got the house. I wanted him to have a house, and a yard, and neighbors. Everyone said I was crazy, that I'd never be able to do it, that I'd be sorry I'd given everything up to raise a child on my own. But I'm not sorry. He's the best thing that ever happened to me. And I've done a good job. Keenan's happy, and he's bright and funny and wonderful. We have a good life, and I know I can make it even better. I haven't needed anyone. And… Oh, God, I'm in love with you.''

The hand he'd lifted awkwardly to pat her head froze. ''What?''

''Oh, what a mess. What a mess.'' She plucked a tiny sock out of the laundry basket and wiped her eyes. ''Maybe it's just hormones. It could be, you know. But I walked in and you were sleeping with him on the couch. It was so sweet. Then you were kissing me and everything went crazy. Then you're out in the yard looking so smug and male, showing Keenan how to hit that silly ball. And you're eating pancakes and looking at me. I can hardly breathe when you're looking at me.''

Somewhere along the line, his mind had gone blank. ''I think I missed a step.''

''No, you didn't.'' She sniffled and struggled to get herself under control. ''I've just taken too many. It's my fault. You've been nice to Keenan, and you've been honest with me.'' She sighed, dropped the damp sock in her lap. ''Believe me, I know my emotions are my responsibility.'' Because he was still staring at her, like a man who'd just had the friendly family dog lunge for his throat, she smiled. ''I'm sorry, Coop. I shouldn't have dumped all that on you. I didn't even know it was all bottled up.''

This time he took a step back. ''Zoe, I like the kid. Who wouldn't? And I'm attracted to you. But—''

''There's no need to explain.'' Steady now, she rose. ''Really, there isn't. I don't expect anything from you, and I'm sorry if I made you uncomfortable. But I feel a lot better.'' And, oddly enough, she did. ''When I go to bed with you, we'll understand each other.''

''When you—''

''I think we both know that's going to happen,'' she said calmly. ''We both want it to, and it's smarter to face that than to live with all this tension. Keenan's been wanting to spend the night with a friend of his. I'll arrange it.'' She laughed a little at Coop's expression. ''It's a little hard to be spontaneous with a four-year-old around. I hope you don't mind planning out a night together.''

''No, I mean, I don't— God, Zoe.''

''If you'd rather not, or if you want some time to decide, that's all right.''

He studied her face, felt that same greedy tug, and a flare of something entirely different. Entirely new. ''No, I want you. Whenever.''

''How about Monday night?''

''I've got a twilight doubleheader on Monday.'' He couldn't believe he was standing here planning out a wild night of love like a dentist's appointment.

''Ah... Wednesday?''

He nodded. ''Wednesday's good for me. Do you want to go out somewhere?''

It was sweet, she thought, really sweet of him to ask. "It's not necessary." She laid a hand on his cheek. "I don't need flowers and candlelight. I'll come upstairs after Keenan's settled."

"Good. Fine. I...better get back to work."

"Do you still want to have Keenan tomorrow?"

"Yeah, no problem. Tell him to come on up." Coop backed toward the door as Zoe began folding laundry again. "I guess I'll see you."

She listened to him walk up the steps. He was certainly a mistake, she told herself. But she'd made others. Life got too mundane when you avoided all the wrong turns.

Chapter 7

"He shoots, he scores!" Coop made appropriate crowd noises as Keenan dunked the basket.

"I can do it again! I can, okay?" From his perch on Coop's shoulders, Keenan swung his sneakered feet.

"Okay, you've drawn the foul." Coop scooped the palm-sized ball up and passed it into Keenan's eager hands. "It's game point, kid, ten seconds to play. This free throw is all-or-nothing. Got it?"

"Got it!"

"A hush falls over the crowd as Fleming steps up to the line. He's played the game of his life tonight, but it all comes down to this one shot. He eyes the basket. You eyeing the basket?"

"Eyeing it," Keenan said, with his tongue caught between his teeth.

"He sets...and shoots." Coop winced as the little rubber ball circled the rim, then watched through squinted eyes as it tipped in and dropped through the net.

"And the crowd goes wild!" Coop danced around the sofa while Keenan hooted and clapped on his shoulders. When he dumped the boy on the cushions of the sofa, Keenan let go with one of the rolling belly laughs that always made Coop grin. "You're a natural."

"You shoot it, Coop! You!"

Obliging, Coop executed a quick turnaround jump shot. This wasn't such a bad way to spend a rainy afternoon, he decided. And it helped keep his mind off how he was going to spend the rainy night ahead.

It was Wednesday.

"Okay, time out. I've got to finish up my piece on the track meet."

"Are we going to go to the paper again? It's neat there."

"Not today. I'm going to fax it in when it's done. You watch some tube." Coop hit the remote, then handed it over.

"Can I get a drink?"

"Yeah, there's some of that juice your mom sent up for you. Stay out of trouble, right?"

"Right."

When Coop headed into his office, Keenan scrambled up from the couch. He liked it best when he got to stay with Coop after school. They always got to do something neat, and Coop never asked if he'd washed his hands or said too many cookies would spoil his appetite.

Best of all, he liked when Coop picked him up. It was different than when his mother did. He liked when she held him, nuzzled him after his bath or rocked him when he had a bad dream. But Coop smelled different, and felt different.

He knew why, Keenan thought as he wandered into the kitchen. It was because Coop was a daddy instead of a mom.

He liked to pretend Coop was his daddy, and figured that maybe if he didn't do anything bad, Coop wouldn't go away.

After a couple of tugs, Keenan had the refrigerator open. He was proud that Coop had hung the pictures he had drawn for him on the door. He peered inside, saw the jug of juice his mother had bought for him. And the green bottles Coop liked.

"B-E-E-R," Keenan said to himself. He remembered that he'd asked Coop if he could have a taste from the bottle, and that Coop had told him he couldn't until he was big. After Coop had let him sniff the beer, Keenan had been glad he wasn't big yet.

There was a new bottle in the fridge today, and Keenan knit his brow and tried to recognize the letters. *C-H-A-R-D-O-N—* There were too many letters to read, so he lost interest.

He took out the jug, gripping it manfully and setting it on the floor. Humming to himself, he dragged a chair over to get cups from the cabinet. One day he'd be as tall as Coop and wouldn't need to stand on a chair. He leaned forward on his toes.

The crash and the howl had Coop leaping up, rapping his knee hard against the desk. Papers scattered as he raced out of the office and into the kitchen.

Keenan was still howling. A chair was overturned, juice was glugging cheerfully onto the floor, and the refrigerator was wide open. Coop splashed through the puddle and scooped Keenan up.

"Are you hurt? What'd you do?" When his only answer was another sob, he stood Keenan on the kitchen table and searched for blood. He imagined gaping wounds, broken bones.

"I fell down." Keenan wriggled back into Coop's arms.

"Okay, it's okay. Did you hit your head?"

"Nuh-uh." With a sniffle, Keenan waited for the kisses he expected after a hurt. "I fell on my bottom." Keenan's lip poked out. "Kiss it."

"You want me to kiss your— Come on, kid, you're joking."

The lip trembled, another tear fell. ''You gotta kiss where it hurts. You gotta, or it won't get better.''

''Oh, man.'' Flummoxed, Coop dragged a hand through his hair. He was desperately relieved that no blood had been spilled, but if anyone, anyone, found out what he was about to do, he'd never live it down. He turned Keenan around and gave the little rump a quick kiss. ''Does that do it?''

''Uh-huh.'' Keenan knuckled his eyes, then held out his arms. ''Will you pick me up?''

''Yeah.'' He didn't feel as ridiculous as he'd expected when the boy's arms went around his neck. ''Okay now?''

With his head resting on Coop's shoulder, he nodded. ''I didn't mean to do it. I spilled all the juice.''

''No big deal.'' Hardly realizing he did so, Coop turned his head to brush his lips over Keenan's hair. Something was shifting inside him, creaking open.

''You aren't mad at me? You won't go away?''

''No.'' What the hell was going on? Coop wondered as unexplored and unexpected emotions swirled inside him. ''No, I'm not going anywhere.''

''I love you,'' Keenan said, with the simple ease of a child.

Coop closed his eyes and wondered how a grown man was supposed to handle falling for a four-year-old boy.

Well, here she was, Zoe thought as she stood at the bottom of the steps leading to Coop's apartment. All she had to do was go upstairs, open the door and start an affair. Her stomach clenched.

Silly to be nervous, she told herself, and climbed the first step. She was a normal woman with normal needs. If her emotions were too close to the surface, she would deal with it. It was much more difficult to be hurt when you had no expectations.

She'd had expectations once, but she knew better now.

This was simply a physical attraction between two single, healthy people. She'd nearly backed down a step before she forced herself to move forward. All the practical details had been seen to. Her son was safely tucked away for the night at his sleep-over. She'd arranged for birth control—that wasn't an oversight she would make again.

No regrets, she promised herself as she lifted a hand to knock. She knew how useless they were.

He answered so quickly, she nearly jumped. Then they stood and stared at each other.

She'd worn a dress, one of those thin, breezy sundresses designed to make a man give thanks for the end of winter. Her hair was loose, falling over thin raspberry-colored straps and bare, peach-toned shoulders. There were nerves in her eyes.

''Hi.'' He glanced down to the cordless phone she held. ''Expecting a call?''

"What? Oh." She laughed, miserably self-conscious. "No, I just don't like to be out of touch when Keenan's not home."

"He's all settled at his pal's?"

"Yeah." She stepped inside, set the phone on the counter. "He was so excited, he—" She broke off when her sandal stuck to the floor.

Coop grimaced. "I guess I missed some of it. We had a spill."

"Oh?"

"The kid took a tumble, sheared off ten years of my life. No blood lost, though. Just a half gallon of orange juice." When she only smiled, he stepped to the refrigerator. Why in hell was he babbling? "Want some wine?"

"That would be nice." Why, he's as nervous as I am, she realized, and she loved him for it. "Keenan's having a wonderful time staying with you. I have to study the sports pages now just to keep up with what he's talking about."

"He catches on fast."

"So do I. Go ahead," she said as he handed her a glass of wine, "Ask me about stats. I know all about RBIs and ERAs." She took a sip, then gestured with her glass. "I think the Orioles would have taken the second game of that doubleheader the other night if they'd put in a relief pitcher in the second inning."

His lips twitched. "Do you?"

"Well, the starter had lost his stuff, obviously. The guy who was announcing—"

"The play-by-play man."

"Yes, he said so himself."

"So, you watched the game."

"I watch 'Sesame Street,' too. I like to keep up with Keenan's interests." She trailed off when Coop reached out to twine a lock of her hair around his finger.

"He's got a thing for dinosaurs, too."

"I know, I've checked a half dozen books out of the library. We've—" The fingers trailed over her shoulder. "We've been down to the natural history museum twice."

She set the glass aside and fell into his arms.

He kissed her as though he'd been starved for her taste. The impact was fast, deep, desperate. The little purring sounds that vibrated in her throat had his muscles turning into bundles of taut wire.

"I wasn't sure you'd come."

"Neither was I. I—"

"Can't think of anything but you," he said as he swept her off her feet. "I thought we'd take this slow."

"Let's not," she murmured, pressing her lips to his throat as he carried her into the bedroom.

She had a quick impression of Spartan neatness and simple masculine colors and lines before they tumbled onto the bed.

Neither of them was looking for patience. They rolled together, a tangle of limbs grasping, groping, glorying. The sheer physicality of it, flesh to flesh, mouth to mouth, had Zoe's head reeling. Oh, she wanted to be touched like this, to feel so desperately like a woman, with a man's hand streaking over her, with his lips savoring every thud of her pulse.

So she lost herself. No more nerves, no more fears. And if she loved, it only made the joy of mating more lovely.

She was every man's fantasy. Stunningly responsive, breathlessly aggressive. And so beautiful, he thought. Undraped, the exquisite body was so slim, so perfect, he couldn't believe it had ever carried a child. In the gilded light of dusk, her face was elegant, heart-stopping. Whenever he touched, wherever he touched, he could see the bold echo of her pleasure reflected in her eyes.

He watched those eyes glaze over, felt her body tense, heard her strangled cry of release. Swamped with the power of it, he drove her upward again until they were both panting for air, until she reared up from the bed and wrapped herself around him.

Damp skin slid over damp skin, hungry mouth sought hungry mouth. They rolled over the bed again, moaning, quivering. Then his hands gripped hers, and his mouth crushed her mouth. And he thrust inside her, hard and deep.

She felt the sensation as if it were a lance through her system, painful, glorious. For an instant, neither of them moved, they just stayed tensed and shuddering on the edge.

Then it was all movement, all speed, a wild race that ended with them both plunging deliriously over the finish line.

It wasn't exactly the way he'd imagined, Coop thought. They were sprawled across his bed, Zoe curled against him. The light was nearly gone, and the room was full of shadows.

He'd imagined they would progress to the bedroom by stages. They were both adults and had known that was the ultimate goal, but he'd thought they would move slowly.

Then she'd been standing there smiling, the nerves shining in her eyes… He'd never wanted anything or anyone more in his life.

Still, he thought she deserved more than a quick tussle, however rewarding. But the night was young.

He flexed his arm to bring her head a little closer, brushed his lips over her temple. "Okay?"

"Mmm… At the very least." Her body felt golden. She was surprised her skin didn't glow in the dark.

"I rushed you a little."

"No, perfect timing."

He began to trail a finger up and down her arm. He wanted her again. Good God, his system was already churning to life. A little control, Coop, he ordered himself. "You're going to stay?"

She opened her eyes, looking into his. "Yes."

"I'm going to go get the wine."

"That's good." She sighed as he left the bed. She'd forgotten how to deal with the after, she realized. Or with the before and during, for that matter, she thought with a wry smile. Though she thought she'd done pretty well so far.

She hadn't known how much had been bottled up inside her. Or just how much she'd needed to feel like a woman again. But then, she hadn't known she could love again.

She shifted, slipping under the tangled sheets, automatically lifting them to her breasts when Coop came back with the wine and glasses.

The sight of her in his bed shot to his loins, with a quick detour through the heart. He said nothing, pouring wine, offering her a fresh glass and settling beside her.

"Why haven't you been with anyone?" The moment the question was out, he wished for a rusty knife to hack off his tongue. "Sorry, none of my business."

"It's all right." Because I haven't fallen in love with anyone before you, she thought. But that wasn't what he wanted to hear, she knew. Nor was it really what he'd asked.

"You want to know about Keenan's father."

"None of my business," he repeated. "Sorry, it's the reporter in me."

"It was a long time ago—a lifetime ago. I don't mind telling you. I grew up in New York. I think I mentioned that my mother's an actress. I was the result of a second marriage. She's had five. So far."

"Five?"

Zoe chuckled into her wine, sipped. "Clarice falls in love and changes husbands the way some women change hairstyles. My father lasted about four years before they parted amicably. Clarice always has friendly divorces. I didn't see much of him, because he moved to Hollywood. He does commercials and voice-overs mostly. Anyway, I think she was on husband number four when I was in high school. He had some pull with the Towers Modeling Agency. They're pretty big."

"I've heard of them."

"Well, he got me in. I started doing some shoots. And I caught on."

"That's it," Coop said, interrupting her. "I knew I'd seen your face before."

She moved her shoulders. "Five, six years ago, it was hard to avoid it. I did twenty covers in one month, the year after I graduated school."

"Cover of *In Sports,* swimsuit edition."

She smiled. "You've got a good memory. That was six years ago."

He remembered the long, sand-dusted legs, the lush wet red excuse for a bathing suit, the laughing, seductive face. He gulped down wine. "It was a hell of a shot."

"And a long, grueling shoot. Anyway, I was making a lot of money, getting a lot of press, going to lots of parties. I met Roberto at one of them."

"Roberto." Coop grimaced at the sound of the name.

"Lorenzi. Tennis player. You might have heard of him."

"Lorenzi? Sure—took the French Open three years ago in straight sets, then blew Wimbledon in the semis. He's got a bad attitude and likes to race cars and chase women on the side. Hasn't been seeded above twenty-fifth in the last two years. Got some bad press this spring when he tipped back too many vinos and punched out a photographer." Coop started to drink, stopped. "Lorenzi? He's Keenan's father? But he's—"

"A womanizer?" Zoe supplied. "A creep, a rich, spoiled egotist? I know—now. What I saw then was a gorgeous, charming man who sent me roses and jetted me off to Monte Carlo for intimate dinners. I was dazzled. He told me he loved me, that he adored me, worshiped me, he couldn't live without me. I believed him, and we became lovers. I thought, since he was my first, he'd be my only. Anyway, I didn't realize he was already getting tired of me when I found out I was pregnant. When I told him, he was angry, then he was very calm, very reasonable. He assumed I'd want an abortion and agreed to pay all the expenses, even to make the arrangements."

"A real prince."

"It was a logical assumption," Zoe said calmly. "I had a career on fast forward, in a field that wouldn't wait while I put on weight and suffered from morning sickness. He, of course, had no intention of marrying me, and thought, rightly enough, that I knew the rules of the game. I did know them," she said quietly. "But something had changed when the doctor confirmed the pregnancy. After the disbelief, the panic, even the anger, I felt good. I felt right. I wanted the baby, so I quit my job, moved away from New York and read everything I could get my hands on about parenting."

"Just like that?"

"Well, there were some scenes, some dire predictions, and a lot of anger, but that's how it worked. Roberto and I parted less than amicably, but with the agreement that he would stay out of my life and I would stay out of his."

"What have you told Keenan?"

"It's tough." And it never failed to make her feel guilty. "So far I've just told him his father had to go away, that he wasn't going to come back. He's happy, so he doesn't ask a lot of questions."

"Are you? Happy?"

"Yes." She smiled and touched his cheek. "I am. All my life I wanted a home, a family, something solid and settled. I didn't even know it until Keenan. He changed my life."

"No urge to go back and smile for the camera?"

"Oh, no. Not even a twinge."

He cupped a hand behind her neck, studying her. "It's such a face," he murmured. Right now he liked the idea of having it all to himself.

Chapter 8

The concept of car pools obviously had been devised by someone with a foul and vicious sense of humor. Having lived most of his life in cities where public transportation or a quick jog would get a man from his home to his office, Coop had never experienced the adult version.

But he'd heard rumors.

Arguments, petty feuds, crowded conditions, spilled coffee.

After a week as designated driver, Coop had no doubt the kiddie version was worse. Infinitely worse.

"He's pinching me again, Mr. McKinnon. Brad's pinching me."

"Cut it out, Brad."

"Carly's looking at me. I told her to stop looking at me."

"Carly, don't look at Brad."

"I'm going to be sick. Mr. McKinnon, I'm going to be sick right now."

"No, you're not."

Though Matthew Finney made gagging noises that had the other kids screeching, Coop gritted his teeth and kept driving. Matt threatened to be sick twice a day unless he rode in the front seat. After five miserable days Coop had his number. But that did very little to soothe his nerves.

Keenan, who had waited all week for his turn in the front, swiveled in his seat to make monster faces at Matt. This incited a small riot of elbow jabs, howls, screaming giggles and shoves.

"Keenan, turn around!" Coop snapped. "You guys straighten up back there. Cut it out! If I have to stop this car..." He trailed off, shuddered. He'd sounded like his own mother. Now Coop was afraid *he* would be sick. "Okay, first stop. Matt, scram."

Fifteen minutes later, his back seat thankfully empty, Coop pulled into the drive and rested his throbbing head on the steering wheel. "I need a drink."

"We got lemonade," Keenan told him.

"Great." He reached over to unbuckle Keenan's seat belt. All he needed was a pint of vodka to go with it.

"Can we go swimming again soon?"

The idea of taking a herd of screaming kids back to the community pool anytime within the next century had a stone lodging in Coop's heart. "Ask your mother."

Coop started to look in the back seat and realized he couldn't face it. Earlier in the week he'd made that mistake, and discovered wads of chewing gum on the rug, cookie crumbs everywhere, and a mysterious green substance smeared on the seat.

In his weakened state, even a candy wrapper was likely to tip the balance.

"Yoo-hoo!" Mrs. Finkleman stripped off her flowered garden gloves and headed across the lawn in a flowing tent dress and electric-blue sandals. "How was your swim, little man?"

"We had races, and Brad dunked Carly and made her cry even though Coop told him not to, and I can hold my breath underwater for twelve seconds."

"My goodness." She laughed and ruffled Keenan's hair. "You'll be in the Olympics next." Her shrewd eyes took in Coop's haggard face. "You look a little frazzled, Coop. Keenan, why don't you run in and tell Mr. Finkleman you want a piece of that cherry cobbler he baked today?"

"Okay!" He tugged on Coop's hand. "Do you want some? Do you wanna come?"

"I'll pass. You go ahead."

Mrs. Finkleman chuckled as Keenan darted away and scrambled up the steps. "Little angel. We'll keep him entertained for a couple of hours—or he'll keep us entertained. You look like you could use a few minutes in a quiet room."

"Padded room," Coop muttered. "How does anyone survive kids?"

"It's easier if you go through the stages with them. Once you've walked the floor all night with a colicky baby, nothing much fazes you." She sighed. "Except science projects. Science projects always took me to the edge. And that first driving lesson." She shook her head at the memory. "That can bring you to your knees." She beamed and patted his arm. "But there's years yet to worry about that. And you've been doing a fine job. Why, Harry and I were just saying how nice it is that Zoe and Keenan have a man in their lives. Not that Zoe hasn't been handling everything. Raising that sweet-natured boy all alone, and working two jobs and tending the house. But it does my heart good to see you and that little angel playing ball in the yard, or the way Zoe lights up when you're around. You make a lovely little family. Now, you go and take a nice nap. We'll keep an eye on your boy."

"I'm not— He's not—" But even as Coop stammered, she was drifting away.

Family? he thought as a ball of ice formed in his stomach. They weren't a family. Oh, no, he promised himself as he walked around the house to his steps. He hadn't taken that on.

He liked the kid, sure. What wasn't to like? And he was damn near nuts about the mother. But that didn't make them a family. That didn't make things permanent. Maybe he'd volunteered to spend time with the kid, taught him a few things about ball, pitched him a few, but that didn't make him Daddy.

He headed straight for the refrigerator, popped the top off a beer and took a long pull.

Sure, maybe he enjoyed having the kid around, and Lord knows he enjoyed being with Zoe. He'd even been sort of pleased when a woman at the pool mistook Keenan for his and commented on what a handsome son he had. But that didn't mean he was going to start thinking about family health insurance or college funds.

He was single. He liked being single. It meant coming and going as he pleased, planning all-night poker games, spending all day with the sports channel blaring.

He liked working in his own space—that was why he did the bulk of his writing at home, rather than at the paper. He didn't like people messing with his things or structuring his time or planning outings.

Family life—as he remembered from his childhood—was lousy with outings.

No way was he changing his nice comfortable existence to accommodate a family.

So he'd made a mistake, Coop decided, and stretched out on the couch with his beer. He'd given Zoe and the kid a little too much of his time, a little too much of his attention. It hadn't been anything he didn't want to give, but he could see now that the gesture could be misconstrued. Particularly since Zoe had once brought up the *L* word. Only once, he reminded himself, and he'd like to think that had just been a woman thing.

Still, if he didn't back off, they might start to depend on him. He shifted uncomfortably as the idea flitted through his mind that he might also come to depend on them.

It was time to reestablish himself as the tenant upstairs.

Keenan raced out of the house next door the minute his mother pulled her car in the drive.

"Hi, Mama, hi! I held my breath for twelve seconds underwater!"

Zoe caught him on the fly and swung him twice. "You must be hiding gills in there," she said, tickling his ribs. "Hi, Mrs. Finkleman."

"Hi yourself. We've had ourselves a fine hour. I sent Coop up for a nap when they got home. He looked like he'd had a rough day."

"Thanks." She kissed Keenan's waiting lips, then smacked her own. "Mmm... Cherries."

"Mr. Finkleman baked them, and they were good."

"I bet. Did you say thank you?"

"Uh-huh. Matt almost throwed up in Coop's car."

"Threw up," Zoe said as she carried Keenan inside.

"Uh-huh. 'Cause it was my turn to ride in the front. I had the best time, and Coop helped me to swim without my bubbles. He said I was a champ."

"That's just what you are." She collapsed with him on a chair. The idea of fixing dinner, changing into her uniform and serving drinks for six hours loomed heavily. "Give me a hug," she demanded, then soothed herself with some nuzzling. "Definitely a champion hugger. Why don't you come in the kitchen and tell me what else you did today while I fix dinner?"

A half hour later, as Zoe was draining pasta and Keenan was entertaining himself with crayons and paper on the kitchen floor, she heard the sound of Coop's feet on the stairs. Her heart sped up. The normal, healthy reaction made her smile. Imagine, she thought, believing herself immune to men.

She left the pasta draining in the sink and went to the back door just as he came to the foot of the steps.

"Hi."

"How's it going?" Coop jingled the keys in his pocket. Did she look all lit up? he wondered. She was smiling, and despite the shadows of fatigue under them, her eyes did have the prettiest lights in them.

"I was just going to call upstairs. I thought you'd

like some dinner after a hard day at the pool.'' She opened the screen door and leaned out to kiss him. The smile dimmed a bit when he eased back. ''It's just chicken and pasta.''

It smelled nearly as good as she did. He glanced inside—the homey scene, cluttered counters, fresh flowers, steam rising from a pan on the stove, the child sprawled on the floor, the pretty woman offering him food and kisses.

A definite trap.

''Thanks, but I'm on my way out.''

''Oh. I thought you had a couple hours before game time.'' She laughed at his arched brow. ''I guess I've been paying more attention to the sports scene. Baltimore versus Toronto, game one of three.''

''Yeah.'' When she starts to take an interest in *your* interests, she's really shutting the cage door. ''I've got some stuff to do.''

''Can I go with you?'' Keenan dashed to the door to tug on Coop's slacks. ''Can I go to the game? I like watching them with you best.''

Coop could almost hear the locks clicking into place. ''I've got too much to do,'' he said, with an edge to his voice that had Keenan's lips quivering. ''Look, it's not just a game, it's my job.''

''You said I was good luck.''

''Keenan.'' Zoe put her hand on her son's shoulder to draw him back, but her eyes stayed on Coop's.

"Did you forget Beth was coming over to stay with you tonight? She'll be here soon, and you're going to watch a tape of your favorite movie."

"But I wanna—"

"Now go wash your hands for dinner."

"But—"

"Go on now."

The way Keenan's face crumpled would have softened an ogre's heart. Dragging his feet, he headed out of the kitchen.

"I can't take him with me everywhere...." Coop began defensively.

"Of course not. He's just overtired. I couldn't have let him go, in any case." She hesitated, wishing she could ignore her instincts. "Is everything all right?"

"Everything's fine." He didn't know why he shouted it. He didn't know why he felt like something slimy stuck to the bottom of a shoe. "I have a life, you know. I don't need kids climbing up my back or you fixing me dinner. And I don't have to explain myself."

Her eyes turned very cool, her face very composed. "You certainly don't. I appreciate you helping me out the past couple of weeks. Let me know if I can return the favor."

"Look, Zoe—"

"I've got to get dinner on the table, or I'll be late for work." She let the screen door slam between them. "Enjoy the game."

She knew exactly how long he continued to stand there while she worked at the stove. Knew exactly when he turned and walked away.

It wasn't unexpected, she reminded herself. This backing away was typical, even understandable. Perhaps it had taken Coop a few weeks to completely comprehend that she didn't come as a single. She was part of a pair, a ready-made family, with its share of responsibilities and problems and routines.

And he was opting out.

He might not even know it yet, she thought, but he was in the first stages of a full retreat.

Her eyes blurred, her chest heaved. Resolutely she choked the tears back. She would indulge herself with a nice long cry later, she promised. But for now she had a little boy to soothe.

When he came back in, she crouched down until they were eye-to-eye.

"You had a good time with Coop today, didn't you?"

Keenan sniffled, nodded.

"And he's taken you a lot of places. You've had fun, and done a lot of new things."

"I know."

"You should be grateful for that, baby, instead of pouting because you can't have more."

She straightened again and hoped she could take her own advice.

Chapter 9

"You're spending a lot of time around here." Ben edged a hip onto the corner of Coop's desk. All around Coop's cubicle phones rang, keyboards clattered.

"So?" Without taking his eyes from the computer screen, Coop hammered out the draft of his weekly column.

"I just figured you had it made in that apartment of yours. I mean, great location." He thought of Zoe. "Great view. You didn't spend as much time in here when you lived downtown."

"I needed a change of scene."

"Yeah." Ben snorted and picked up a baseball from Coop's desk. "Trouble in paradise?"

"I don't know what you're talking about. And I've got a column to write."

"Pretty obvious the last few weeks that you've been stuck on the landlady." He tossed the ball from one hand to the other. "I mean, when a man hauls a kid around, buys little baseball jerseys, it follows that he's hooking a line into Mom."

Coop's eyes flashed up. "I like the kid, okay? I don't have to use a four-year-old to get a woman. The kid's cool."

"Hey, I got nothing against rug rats. Might even have a few of my own one day. The thing is, when a woman's got one, a man has to play Daddy if he wants the inside track."

"Who says I have to play at anything to get a woman?"

"Not me. But it was you who couldn't shoot hoop last week because you were taking the family to the aquarium." Ben winked, set the ball down. "Still, I bet you scored better than I did." Ben jerked back as Coop lunged for his throat.

"It's not like that," Coop said between his teeth.

"Hey, hey. Just yanking your chain. I wouldn't have made any cracks if I'd known you were serious about her."

Coop's grip loosened. "I didn't say I was serious. I said it wasn't like that."

"Whatever you say."

Disgusted with himself, Coop dropped back in his chair. He and Ben had been riding each other about women for better than five years. No reason to overreact, he thought. Or to make a fool of himself. "Sorry. I've got a lot on my mind."

"Forget it. What you need's a distraction. You coming to the poker game tonight?"

"Yeah."

"Good. Losing money should put you back on track."

Something had to, Coop thought as he sat back alone in his cubicle to stare at his screen. For the past three days he'd slept little, eaten less, and gone around in a constant state of flux.

Because he was avoiding the issue, he decided. Opting to bunt, when he should be swinging away. The only solution to getting his life back in order was to face the problem head-on.

He flicked off his terminal.

The beautiful thing about an afternoon off, Zoe thought, was the solitude. No customers to talk to, no orders to fill. It meant she didn't have to be salesclerk, or waitress, or Mom, or anything but Zoe.

Sitting on the back stoop, she struggled to understand the assembly instructions for the new barbecue grill she'd bought. She was going to surprise Keenan with hamburgers.

She liked the quiet—her kind of quiet, which meant there was music throbbing from the kitchen radio. She liked the loneliness—her kind of loneliness, which meant Keenan would dash toward her shortly with open arms and chattering voice.

She knew the upstairs apartment was empty, and she tried not to think about that. Tried not to think about the fact that Coop had been away more than he'd been home in the last few days.

Foolish of her to have thought he was different. He'd wanted her, he'd had her, and now he'd lost interest. Well, she had wanted him, so they were even there. If her heart was suffering it would pass. It had passed before. She and Keenan could get along fine on their own. Just like always.

Her screwdriver slipped, scraped her knuckles, had her swearing.

"What the hell are you doing?"

Eyes hot, she looked up at Coop. "Baking a cake. What does it look like I'm doing?"

"You can't put something together if you're going to spread parts all over the damn place." Automatically he bent down to organize. She rapped his hand away with the rubber grip of the screwdriver.

"I don't need you to put things together for me. I'm not some poor helpless female who needs a man to pick up the slack. I managed just fine before you came along."

Stung, he rammed his hands in his pockets. "Fine. Do it yourself."

"I am doing it myself. I like doing it myself."

‘‘Terrific. And when the thing topples over, you won’t have anyone else to blame.’’

‘‘That’s right.’’ She blew her hair out of her eyes. ‘‘I accept when something’s my fault.’’ She picked up a wrench and locked a bolt in place. ‘‘Do you plan to hover over me all afternoon?’’

‘‘I want to talk to you.’’

‘‘So talk.’’

He had it well planned. He was a writer, after all. ‘‘I realize the way I’ve been hanging around with you and the kid—’’

‘‘His name is Keenan,’’ Zoe said between her teeth.

‘‘I know what his name is. The way I’ve been hanging around the last few weeks might give the wrong impression.’’

‘‘Oh, really?’’ She looked up again, tapping the wrench against her palm.

‘‘He’s a great kid, he kind of grows on you. I’ve gotten a kick out of spending time with him.’’

Though she hated herself for it, Zoe softened. She understood that he was genuinely fond of Keenan. That only made it all the more difficult. ‘‘Hc likes spending time with you. It’s been good for him.’’

‘‘Well, yeah, on the one hand. On the other, I started thinking that he—that you—that both of you might get the wrong idea. I mean, tossing a ball around or taking him to a game, that’s cool. I just don’t want him thinking it’s like—permanent.’’

"I see." She was calm now, frigidly so. It would help keep the hurt in check. "You're afraid he might begin to see you as a father figure."

"Well, yeah. Kind of."

"That's natural enough. But then, he spends a lot of time with Mr. Finkleman, too, and with Billy Bowers down the street."

"Finkleman's old enough to be his grandfather, and the Bowers kid is eighteen." Coop backed off, realizing there was a touch of jealousy in the defense. "And they don't have the same sort of thing going with you."

She arched both brows. "Thing?"

"Relationship," he said tightly. "Whatever the hell you want to call it. Damn it, we only slept together once."

"I'm aware of that." Carefully she set the wrench aside. It would give her only momentary pleasure to heave it at his head.

"That came out wrong," he said, furious with himself. "It sounded like it didn't mean anything. It did, Zoe." A great deal, he was afraid. A very great deal. "It's just that..."

"Now you're terrified that Keenan and I will trap you into a family. That you'll wake up one morning and be Daddy, with a wife and a mortgage and a small boy who needs attention."

"Yes. No. Something like that." He was burying

himself, he realized, and he suddenly didn't know why. "I just want to make myself clear."

"Oh, I think you have. Perfectly." She rubbed her hands on her knees as she studied him. "You needn't worry, Coop. I advertised for a tenant, not a father for my child, or a husband for myself. I slept with you because I wanted to, not because I thought I could lure you to the altar."

"I didn't mean it like that." Frustrated, he dragged a hand through his hair. However well he'd planned this little scene, it was going all wrong. "I wanted you. I still do. But I know how badly you were let down before. I don't want to hurt you, Zoe. Or the kid. I just don't want you thinking I'd slide into the gap."

The anger came back, one swift wave of it that reddened her vision. She was on her feet before either of them realized she'd moved. "Keenan and I don't have a gap. We're a family, as real and as complete and as full a family as any could be." She jabbed the wrench at his chest. "Just because Daddy doesn't make three doesn't mean we're less of a unit."

"I didn't mean—"

"I'll tell you what you mean. You see a woman and a small boy and you think they're just pining away for some big strong man to come along and fulfill them. Well, that's bull. If I needed a man, I'd have one. And if I thought Keenan needed a father to make him happy, I'd find him one. And," she continued, advancing and giving him another jab, ''if you think you're at the head of some fictional list, you're wrong. Maybe I'm in love with you, but that's not enough. It's not just me, and it's not just you. Keenan comes first. When and if I want a father for Keenan, he'll be someone with compassion and patience, someone willing to adjust his life to make room for my son. So relax, Cooper. You're in the clear.''

''I didn't come here to fight with you.''

''Good, because I'm finished.''

He grabbed her arm before she could turn away. ''I haven't. I'm trying to be straight with you, Zoe. I care about you, okay? About both of you. I just don't want it to get out of hand.''

''Out of whose hands?'' she retorted. ''Yours? Then that's no problem, is it? Because you know how to hold on to everything inside, really tight. Just keep holding on to it, Coop. Don't worry about me or about Keenan. We'll be fine.'' She jerked her arm free and sat again. Picking up the instruction sheet, she gave it her full attention.

Now why, he wondered, did he feel as though he'd just been rejected? Shaking his head, Coop took a step in retreat. ''As long as we're clear.''

''We are.''

''I've, ah, got a little time, if you want me to help you put that grill together.''

''No thanks. I can do it.'' She slanted him a look.

"I'm going to grill burgers later. You're welcome to join us. Unless you're afraid it will lead to a commitment."

She shoots, he thought wryly, she scores. "Thanks anyway. I've got plans. Maybe I could take a rain check."

"Fine. You know where to find us."

He got drunk. Not sloppily, but thoroughly. When Coop poured himself out of the cab and staggered toward the house, he already knew he'd hate himself in the morning. But it was tonight he had to deal with.

He leaned heavily against Zoe's front door and waited for the porch to settle down under his feet. She might think they'd finished, he told himself blearily, but she was wrong. Dead wrong.

He'd thought of a dozen things he had to say to her.

There was no time like the present.

Lifting a fist, he pounded on the door. "Come on, Zoe." He pounded again. "I know you're in there." He saw a light flick on inside and kept on pounding. "Come on, come on. Open up."

"Coop?" From the other side of the door, Zoe belted her hastily donned robe. She'd been home from the lounge for barely twenty minutes, and in bed for less than five. "It's after two o'clock in the morning. What do you want?"

"I want to talk to you. Let me in."

"We'll talk in the morning."

"You just said it was morning."

When he pounded again, she flicked off the locks. "Stop that—you'll wake Keenan." Furious, she yanked open the door and had the surprise of a hundred-and-seventy-pound male tumbling against her. "Are you hurt? What happened?" The alarm signals that had screamed on shifted when she caught the scent of beer. "You're drunk."

"Mostly." He started to straighten, then lost himself in the smell of her. "God, you feel good. What d'you wash this in?" He nuzzled her hair. "Smells like moonbeams."

"Really drunk," she said with a sigh. "Sit down. I'll get you some coffee."

"Don't want coffee. Doesn't sober you up, only wakes you up. And I'm awake, and I have something to say to you." He drew away then, and discovered he wasn't as steady as he'd hoped. "But I'll sit down." He did, heavily. "Hate getting drunk. Haven't done it like this since I played minor league. Did I tell you I played minor league ball? Triple A."

"No." Baffled, she stood her ground and watched him.

"Right out of high school. Two years. Thought I'd make it to the show. The majors. But I didn't, so I went to college, and now I write about people who did."

"I'm sorry."

"No." He waved that away. "I like writing. Always did. Like watching the games and seeing all the little dramas. If I'd've played, I'd be nearly washed up now. I'm almost thirty-three. Old man for the game." He focused on her, smiled. "You're the most beautiful woman I've ever seen in my life. You know, the kid looks just like you. Look at him, see you. It's spooky. I see you all the time. Minding my own business, and pop! There's your face in my head. What d'ya make of that?"

"I don't know." She wanted to be angry with him, really she did. But he was so foolishly drunk. "Why don't I take you upstairs, Coop? Put you to bed."

"I want you in my bed, Zoe. I want to make love with you. I want to touch you again."

She wanted that, too. Very much. But new lines had been drawn. "You said you wanted to talk to me."

"Do you know what your skin feels like? I can't describe it, it's all soft and smooth and warm. I started thinking about your skin when I was playing poker and getting drunk tonight. I won, too. Took a big pot with a pair of sixes. Pulled in over two hundred and fifty dollars."

"Congratulations."

"But I kept thinking about you. You have this little dimple right here." He nearly poked himself in the eye, then dragged a finger down his cheek to the corner of his mouth. "I kept thinking about that little dimple, and your skin, and those big eyes and killer legs. And I kept thinking how I like to watch you with the kid, like I do sometimes from upstairs, when you don't know. Didn't know that, did you?''

''No,'' she said quietly. ''I didn't.''

''Well, see...'' He gestured wildly. ''You've got this way of running your hand over his hair. It gets to me.'' He shook his head. ''It really gets to me. Keenan loves me, you know. He told me he did. So did you.''

''I know.''

''And I meant everything I said this afternoon.''

''I know.'' Sighing, she walked over to undo his shoelaces.

''Every word, Zoe. I've got my life set, just like I want it.''

''Okay.'' She pried off his shoes, hefted his legs onto the couch.

''So you can stop popping into my head, 'cause it's not changing anything.''

''I'll keep that in mind.''

He was asleep before she bent over and kissed his cheek.

Chapter 10

As hangovers went, Coop knew, this would be a champ. He didn't have to open his eyes, he didn't have to move, not when his head was already beating like the army drum corps.

He wasn't sure how he'd managed to get home and into bed, but the blur of the evening wasn't comforting. Still, he thought it best to wait to tax his brain.

Cautious, close to fearful, he opened his eyes. The little face directly above him had him jerking back, then moaning at the pain.

''Good morning,'' Keenan said cheerfully. ''Did you sleep over?''

''I don't know.'' Coop lifted a hand to his head. ''Where's your mother?''

"She's making my lunch. She said I could come in and look at you if I didn't wake you up. I didn't wake you up, did I? I was really quiet."

"No." Coop closed his eyes again and prayed for oblivion.

"Are you sick? Do you have a tempature?" Keenan laid a small, light hand on Coop's aching forehead. "Mama can make it better. She always makes it better." Very gently, Keenan replaced his hand with a kiss. "Does that help?"

Oh, hell, Coop thought. Even a hangover didn't have a chance against this kid. "Yeah, thanks. What time is it?"

"The big hand's on the ten and the little hand's on the eight. You can sleep in my bed until you're better, and play with my toys."

"Thanks." Coop made the supreme effort and sat up. When his head rolled, he did his best to catch it in his hands. "Keenan, be a pal and ask your mom for some aspirin."

"Okay." He raced off, and the sound of his sneakers pounding the floor had Coop shuddering.

"Headache?" Zoe asked a moment later.

Coop lifted his head. She was still in her robe. The robe he remembered from the night before. He was beginning to remember quite a bit from the night before. "If you're going to yell at me, could you do it later?"

In answer, she held out aspirin and a glass filled with reddish liquid.

"What is it?"

"A remedy from Joe the bartender. He guarantees it'll take the edge off."

"Thanks."

There was a blast of a horn from outside that cut through Coop's skull like a dulled knife. While he was dealing with the shock of that, Keenan came racing back.

"Bye, Mama, bye!" He gave her a smacking kiss, then turned to hug Coop. "Bye."

As the door slammed behind him, Coop gulped down Joe's remedy.

"Do you want coffee?" Zoe ran her tongue around her teeth and tried not to smile. "Some breakfast?"

"You're not going to yell at me?"

"For barging in here, drunk, in the middle of the night? And for passing out on my sofa?" She paused just long enough to make her point. "No, I'm not going to yell at you. I figure you're suffering enough."

"I am, I promise you." He got up to follow her into the kitchen. "Not just physically. I feel like a total jerk."

"You *were* a total jerk." She poured a mug of coffee, set it on the table for him. "My mother's third husband had a fondness for bourbon. He swore eggs the morning after were the cure. How do you want them?"

"Scrambled would be good." He sat gingerly at the table. "I'm sorry, Zoe."

She kept her back to him. "For?"

"For being a jackass yesterday afternoon, and a bigger jackass last night."

"Oh, that." With the bacon frying, she chose a small bowl to scramble eggs in. "I don't imagine it's the first or the last time you'll be one."

"You didn't..." He shifted miserably. "Ah, you didn't tell Keenan I was..."

"Drunk and disorderly?" A half smile on her face, she glanced over her shoulder. "I told him you weren't feeling well and went to sleep on the couch. Which was close enough."

"Thanks. I wouldn't want him to think...you know. I don't make a habit out of it."

"So you said last night." She turned the bacon, whipped the eggs.

He watched her, gradually getting past the astonishment that she wasn't going to rub his nose in the mess he'd made of things. Remembering the afternoon before, when she'd stood up to him with all that pride and fury shining in her eyes. And the other night, when he'd fallen asleep on her couch—the way she'd looked when she slipped the boy from his arms into hers and carried him into bed.

A dozen other pictures, captured in so short a time, flitted through his head, until they were whittled down to one. This one. Zoe standing at the stove, with the morning sun streaming over her tousled hair, her robe flowing down, breakfast smells warming the room.

How could he have thought he didn't want this? Just this. And what did he do now that he knew the truth?

"Food should help." She set the plate in front of him. "I've got to get ready for work."

"Can you— Have you got a minute?"

"I suppose." She poured herself another cup of coffee. "I don't have to be in until ten."

He began to eat while thoughts scrambled in his brain. "This is good. Thanks."

"You're welcome." She leaned back against the counter. "Did you want something else?"

"Yeah." He ate more, hoping eggs equaled courage. Then he put his fork down. It was the ninth inning, he thought, and there were already two outs. "You. I want you."

She smiled a little. "Coop, I doubt you're in any shape for that, and I really have to go to work, so—"

"No, I don't mean that. I mean I do, but not—" He broke off, took a long, deep breath. "I want you to marry me."

"I beg your pardon?"

"I think you should marry me. It's a good idea." Somewhere in the back of his mind, he realized, he'd been working on this all along. He had it figured. "You can quit your night job and go back to school if you want. Or open that flower shop. Whatever. I think that's what we should do."

"Really." Because her hand was unsteady, she set her coffee down. "Well that's very generous of you, Coop, but I don't have to get married to do any of those things. So thanks just the same."

He stared. "No? You're saying no? But you love me. You said it. Twice you said it."

"We can make it three," she said evenly. "Yes, I love you. No, I won't marry you. Now I really have to get ready for work."

"Just a damn minute." Hangover forgotten, he pushed back from the table and rose. "What kind of game is this? You love me, your kid's crazy about me, we're terrific in bed, I even know how to drive a damn car pool, but you won't marry me."

"You're such an idiot. You're such a fool. Do you think because I didn't put up a struggle before I fell into your bed that you can have everything your own way? When you want it, how you want it? Well, you're wrong. And you *are* a jackass."

He winced as she stormed from the room. Strike one, he thought. And he hadn't even seen the pitch.

But the game wasn't over, he thought grimly, until the fat lady sang.

Zoe was still steaming when she came home from work. Of all the arrogant, interfering, self-absorbed idiots she'd ever known, J. Cooper McKinnon took the gold medal. Imagine him telling her that marrying him was a good idea, then ticking off all the advantages she'd gain.

Oh, he thought he was a prize.

One day he's telling her to get any ideas of sneaking him into a relationship out of her head. As if she'd been baiting traps for him. The next he's taking pity on her and offering her a big male helping hand.

She should have bitten it off.

Not once, not once had he said what she would bring to him, what he felt for her, what he wanted. Not once had he brought up the fact that he could or would accept another man's child as his own.

She jerked open the front door, slammed it. He could take his half-baked proposal and sit on it.

"Mama! Hey, Mama!" Keenan zipped into the living room and grabbed her hand. "Come on, come on. We've got a surprise."

"What surprise? What are you doing home, Keenan? You're supposed to be at the Finklemans'."

"Coop's here." He tugged manfully on her hand. "We have a surprise. And we have a secret. And you have to come *now!*"

"All right, I'm coming." She braced herself and let Keenan drag her into the kitchen.

There were flowers, banks of them, vases and baskets overflowing on the counters, on the floor, on the windowsills. There was music, some soft, dreamy classical sonata, on the radio. The table was set, crystal she'd never seen before glinting in the sunlight, a bottle of champagne chilling in a silver bucket. And Coop was standing there, in a neatly pressed shirt and slacks.

"It's a surprise," Keenan announced gleefully. "We made everything look nice so you'd like it. And Mrs. Finkleman said we could use the glasses and the plates. And Mr. Finkleman made his special chicken 'cause it's resistible."

"Irresistible," Coop said, his eyes on Zoe. "You, ah, said you didn't need flowers and candlelight, but I've never taken you out on a date. I thought this was the next-best thing."

"Do you like it, Mama? Do you?"

"Yes, it's very nice." She bent down to kiss Keenan. "Thank you."

"I get to go to the Finklemans' so you can have romance."

"Ah, come on, kid." Coop scooped Keenan up. "Let's get you started. You were supposed to keep quiet about it," he muttered when he carried the boy outside.

"What's romance?"

"I'll tell you later."

Satisfied with that, Keenan draped his arm around Coop's neck. "Are you gonna tell Mama the secret about us all getting married?"

"That's the plan."

"And you'll live with us and you can be my Daddy and that'll be okay?"

"That'll be great. It'll be perfect." He stopped by the fence to press a kiss to Keenan's mouth. "I love you, Keenan."

"Okay." He squeezed his arms hard around Coop's neck. "Bye."

"Bye."

"Yoo-hoo!" Mrs. Finkleman stood at the back door. She sent Coop a wink and an exaggerated thumbs-up sign before whisking Keenan inside.

She was standing pretty much where Coop had left her when he came back. He wasn't sure whether or not that was a good sign.

"So, ready for some champagne?"

"Coop, this is very nice of you, but—"

"Like the flowers?" Nervous as a cat, he popped the cork.

"Yes, they're wonderful, but—"

"I couldn't get them where you work, or I'd have spoiled the surprise. Keenan really gave me a hand setting things up." He handed her the glass, and when she was distracted, he leaned in for a slow, warm kiss. "Hi."

"Coop." She had to wait for her heart to finish its lazy somersault. "I know you must have gone to a lot of trouble—"

"I should have gone to it before. I didn't know I wanted to."

''Oh, Lord.'' She turned away and struggled to get her emotions under control. ''I've given you the wrong impression this time. I don't need the trappings. I don't have to have romantic evenings and—'' she waved toward the tapers on the table, waiting to be lit ''—candlelight.''

''Sure you do. So do I, when they're with you.''

''You're trying to charm me,'' she said unsteadily. ''That's new.''

''You know what I am. The way this house is set up, we've practically been living together for the past month or so. People get to know each other quicker that way than just by socializing. So you know what I am, and you fell for me anyway.''

She took a drink. ''You're awfully smug about it. I told you my feelings are my responsibility, and that holds true. A romantic dinner doesn't change it.''

It looked like strike two, but Coop knew that if he was going to go down, he'd go down swinging. ''So I want to give you a nice evening. Is something wrong with that? I want to do better than propose over scrambled eggs when I've got a hangover.'' His voice had risen, and he bit down on it. ''Damn it, this is my first time, have a little tolerance. No, don't say anything, let me finish this. You don't need me.'' He took another long breath. ''Not for taking care of things, for you or the kid, I mean, for mowing the grass or putting stupid barbecue grills together. What about what I need, Zoe?''

She blinked at him. "Well, that's just it. Don't you see? You made it clear that you don't need or want ties. I come with ties, Coop."

"I made it clear," he muttered. "I didn't make anything clear, because I didn't know. Didn't want to know. I was scared. There. You feel better knowing that?" He glared at her. "I was scared, because I need you. Because I need to see your face and hear your voice and smell your hair. I just need you to be there. And I need to help you mow the grass and put the grill together. I need you to need me back."

"Oh." She shut her eyes. "I like hearing that."

"Then tell me you will." He took her arms until she opened her eyes again. "It's my last swing, Zoe. Marry me."

"I—" Yes. She wanted to say yes. "It's not just me, Coop."

"You think I don't want the kid? God, open your eyes. I'm crazy about him. I fell for him before I fell for you. I want to marry both of you, then maybe have another kid or two so I can start out on the ground floor. We already worked that out."

"You— Who did what?"

He swore, stepped back, shrugged. "I kind of ran it by the kid. I figured I should smooth the way a little, and find out where he stood." When she just stared, he jammed his hands in his pockets. "It didn't seem fair not to bring him into it, since he'd be mine."

"Yours," she murmured, staring blindly into her wine.

"Since you two are a team, it would be sort of like an expansion. Anyway, he's for it. So it's two against one."

"I see."

"Maybe I don't know a lot about the daddy stuff, but I love him. That's a good start."

She looked at him again, looked into his eyes. Her heart opened, flooded. "It's a good one, all right."

"I love you." His hands relaxed in his pockets. "That's the first time I've said that to a woman—except my mother. I love you, Zoe. So why don't you marry me and give me and the kid a break?"

"It looks like I'm outvoted." She lifted a hand to his cheek.

"Is that a yes?"

"That's definitely a yes." She laughed as he swung her into his arms. "Daddy."

"I like the sound of that." He crushed his lips down on hers. "I like it a lot."

* * * * *